Alexander L. Brent is a freelance writer who authored this fictional novel based upon relevant experiences encountered in his life growing up and coming of age in Brooklyn During the 1970's, 80's and 90's. This novel is a labor of love that began in 1999 when he began to examine various portions of his life and put pen to paper and drafted this expose on what living as a youth in the gritty urban center known as Brownsville was like. Alexander Brent has always employed his creative prose to draft poetry and short stories to create a vivid tapestry using the creative word. As a product of New York City Public School System, Alexander Brent was a gifted talented an exceptional student who in later years achieved a bachelor's degree with honors from The College of New Rochelle. At present Alexander Brent is married with three children, has worked for the City of New York for two decades, and currently resides in Bedford Stuyvesant in Brooklyn New York. Alexander Brent has an upcoming work entitled the Book of Reality which is due for publication in 2022.

EPOLOGUE

My life is a coming of age story based on the trials and tribulations of a man-child reared in the belly of the ghetto. As a child facing and adapting to the travails of inner-city violence, to an adolescent struggling with the choice of entering the drug game during the crack-cocaine epidemic of the 1980's. This story addresses the unique experiences faced by young black men everywhere but told from the eyes of one who bore witness to the pain of surviving the Brownsville experience. In his rise from childhood, adolescence and adulthood, this story captures the life of a man faced with a series of test he must overcome in order to gain a deeper understanding of his greatest adversary, himself. My Life is a triumph of the spirit and is a deeply moving testament to the resilience of Black men who face and overcome the fear and uncertainty that effect their lives.

MY LIFE: THE TRIALS AND TRIBULATIONS OF A MAN CHILD IN THE GHETTO

ALEXANDER L. BRENT

Book design by: Word-2-Kindle.com

ISBN 978-1-733 1515-0-4 (paperback)

ISBN 978-1-733 1515-1-1 (eBook)

First paperback edition August 2019

Published by www.Ingram Sparks.com

Library of Congress Control Number: 2019905893

This book was printed in the United States of America

E-mail: lasarbrent@gmail.com

To order additional copies of this book contact: (347)765-6375

PROLOGUE

As I walked through the garbage clustered hallway, the smell of rank urine and feces assaulted my nostrils. The screech of babies could be heard behind the barricaded iron door units. I entered the elevator; an iron tomb encrusted with broken bottles, graffiti and spilled beer and descended to the lobby. My perception was bombarded by the scene unfolding before my eyes. Obese, middle age, gold toothed Aunt Jemima's conversed in pig Latin as they dined on fried pork skins and downed forty-ounce malt liquor. Heavily muscled shirtless thugs crouched in corners chucking dice & smoking weed while barking in unintelligible ghetto vernacular. Children frolicked wildly darting between the medley of thugs, crack heads and welfare queens, their faces covered in mucus and dry food; the stench of poverty was indistinguishable from the warm garbage emanating from the incinerator. Was this a dream or a nightmare? No this was Brownsville, and this was home.

TABLE OF CONTENTS

CHAPTER 1 THE BEGINNIING

I was born and raised in Brownsville Brooklyn. Growing up in the streets of the Ghetto, one of the very first lessons I learned was that only the strong survived. Being reared in a harsh environment, I had to acquire the tools useful for survival. The first rule I learned living in the ghetto was that in order to survive you had to be nice with your hands. Once you became skilled at boxing and street fighting you gained a reputation, others respected your strength and you would be less apt to be tested by your peers in the streets. As boys we would slap box and play corners in the elevator; it was a form of rough and tumble where we would swing, block, push and pull, elbow and kick each other playing for the four corners of the elevator as it descended towards the lobby. It was all for fun, but it was a means of building up courage, strength and toughness. As a black male your street fighting skills had to be honed to a fine razors edge. Back in the days, young boys didn't have access to guns and knives like they do today. It was very important for a ghetto child to be initiated into these urban rites of passage as a way of earning respect and as a means of displaying one's manly prowess. Boys who didn't socialize in this manner were labeled chumps, punk's sissies or pussy's and were often preyed upon by their peers. There were many privileges to those who were high ranking members of the street hierarchy. If you were well known in the streets, you had first pick of the females, you wore the best clothing, and you socialized with all the players, hustlers' ballers and stick up

1

kids; in essence you became a ghetto superstar. I was not one of the ghetto elite, I was a child who came from a very close-knit family. I hung out with my cousins DJ, Keith, Cleveland, Ephraim and K-Swiss. We all began to hang out in our preteen years. But in my earlier years I hung out with my immediate family; namely DJ and Tasha, they were my first cousins. When we were allowed to play outside, we were told we had to return before the streetlamp came on or we would get an ass whooping. With such a short amount of time for play we used to roam Brownsville getting into all types of mischief.

Since the 19th Century Brownsville has been infamous for crime, gangs, poverty and slums. Generally, four miles in length four miles in width, Brownsville housed twelve to thirteen different project complexes. My family hailed from a complex called Langston Hughes. The Towers as they were called, was composed mainly of working-class black folk and veterans who fought during World War II. They were descendants of sharecroppers who migrated from the south during the great exodus in the thirties and the forties to escape Jim Crow only to find urban decay and isolation in the ghettos of the northern cities. In the mist of this urban despair me, DJ and Tasha created an imaginative world of beauty in the confines of the ghetto. While other children our age played skelly, basketball, cee-lo, slap boxed and did nickel and dime hustles, we caught butterflies and bees, flew kites, made go-carts, had water races with ice-cream sticks on sidewalk curbs, and blew bubbles. These types of activities were seemingly normal but in the environment in which we found ourselves these behaviors would have you earmarked as a punk, chump or a sissy. As boys, DJ and I possessed very creative natures. When we were bored, we began to test the boundaries of our playground environment. In a quest for adventure we did a lot of stupid shit. I look back on those years with a sense of nostalgia. Back in those days we used to play a game we coined elevator racing. The object of this game was to out-run the elevator on its way down from the seventeenth floor. We would wait for one or more of our family members to board the elevator.

We would then race down the steps running two steps at a time from the seventeenth to the first floor, to outrun the elevator before it reached the first floor. We were just kids engaging in harmless fun, but unbeknownst to us we were in training to hone our ghetto survival skills. In latter days we would employ our sprinting skills to evade and escape predators seeking to devour, consume and prey upon us as though we were food.

Being from a close-knit family had its advantages. As a child I was cared for and nurtured by every member of my family; my grandmother, grandfather, aunt and my mother. But of all my family members my grandfather was my favorite. He told me stories, he gave me wisdom, he was my only male role model. DJ and I grew up without our fathers. We were raised by our mothers which was the norm in the nineteen seventies. We all lived in a two-bedroom apartment in Langston Hughes on the seventeenth floor. My father was always in and out of jail. I was never taught the fundamentals of what being Black, and male meant in this society and what duties and responsibilities it carried. DJ, his father was killed in a gang fight a couple of months before he was born, leaving him at more of a disadvantage than I. We both adored and feared our grandfather. He was the only stable

3

black male image we were exposed to. He used to tell us stories about his days in the army during the second world war. He was our first hero. He used to show us how strong he was by letting us punch him in his belly until our arms began to tire and our hands were pounding. Then he would laugh out loud and asks us to do it again. He also showed us great feats of agility. He used to wrap his leg around his head and scratch his head with his feet. This was no small feat, even at our tender ages we found this act damn near impossible to do.

Our grandfather was also a chef, a skill he picked up while in the military. He taught us that food should never be wasted. When we ate dinner, he heaped mountains of food on our plate. We used to call them man-plates, because the plate was similar in portion to what a man of twenty-five years of age would eat. He told us if we didn't finish our food that we would get an ass whipping. In those days your mother, your father, grandmother, grandfather and neighbors could whip your ass if you acted out. It was true regarding the old saying, that it takes a village to raise a child.

In those days me and DJ were young strong and adventurous at heart. After school we would do our homework and go outside knowing full well, we had to return by six o'clock. With that in mind we wanted to have as much fun as possible. We began to venture out to other housing projects. During our brief excursions we would encounter other boys we knew were ready and willing to test us. One time during the summer me, DJ, Tasha and Keith went to a swimming pool in Howard projects. At that time Howard projects was run by Puerto Rican gangs and one thing was certain about the Hispanics, if you fucked with one

4

of them, you fucked with them all. We arrived at the pool, but discovered it cost ten cents for entry and none of us had one thin dime. We crept through a hole in the gate at the back of the pool and slid into the pool. The Puerto Ricans dominated the pool, the Blacks were outnumbered four to one. They stood in the middle of the pool waving their flags and shouting Puerto Rican Power. They were bumping, pushing and spitting in niggas faces in order to start some shit. Fights broke out all over the pool between these two warring factions. We thought we had nothing to fear, we were just kid's out to play games and have a good time, unfortunately that was not the case. This Spanish kid ran up on Keith claiming he stole his sneakers. We were suddenly surrounded by a dozen Puerto Ricans. Me DJ and Tasha jumped the gate like professional athletes and did a one-hundred-yard sprint through the projects. They had caught Keith and smacked him up a little bit, but he had the gift of gab, he always knew how to talk his way out of shit. He escaped a serious beat down because he knew a shot caller that looked out for him.

That incident didn't deter us from continuing to explore the ghetto. Me and DJ learned a very important lesson that day. It taught us that family had to stick together. We would fight together, live together and if need be die together. I was my brother's keeper and he was mine. We would never let anyone enter our space. We considered all out siders enemies who could never be trusted. We formed an unwritten code that would serve us well in our later years. It would keep us out of jail, it would keep us from using and selling drugs. It would deter us from being shot, beaten or killed. While other young black men ratted on each other, sold each other out, killed each other over women, money, clothes, and jewelry. We steered clear of all the bullshit by letting no one enter our family circle. This kept us from being influenced by gangs and other negative elements in the community. We were unique because we were able to maintain our individuality and be leaders of ourselves while others in our peer group were slaves to the latest trends, and behaviors that created and dictated the misery of our ghetto existence.

Summer was ending. I dreaded the thought of having to go back to school in the fall to attend the third grade. Meeting new people, seeing new faces, the thought made my stomach quiver. Fall was on the horizon. The neighborhood looked and smelled different. The summer leaves green wet and dripping with dew showered from and all-knowing God began to change from green to a gold auburn. You sensed the change, the once vibrant blocks teeming with shirtless ruffians playing dice and nappy headed rug rats frolicking in the waters of the fire hydrant began to slowly transform as Mother Nature began to lose her beauty to the old age and death of winter.

CHAPTER 2 PUBLIC SCHOOL

Now school was an acutely different environment from the streets. It was more ordered and supervised. In those days' teachers could maintain order by employing corporal punishment. Teachers had the expressed permission from parents to whip that ass if you misbehaved. The year was 1978 I was 8 years old. My mother and hundreds of other women scrambled to register their kids into school. The scene was hectic-you had mothers arguing and kids crying. For many it would be their first time away from home. For their only exposure with the outside world was what they viewed on television; what laid outside of this urban jungle was relatively unknown. Even though I was relatively shy and still attached to my mother, for some reason I was not afraid. I guess that was my adventurous side trying to express itself. I welcomed the experience and didn't utter a complaint as my mother lead me to my classroom and kissed me goodbye.

Public school didn't present much of a problem to me as with other kids because I had home training. To the average ghetto child public schools was a totally alien experience. Most were raised by young single welfare mothers and reared by the television. The average single mother in the ghetto was more preoccupied with providing food clothing and shelter for their children, they didn't have the time nor the energy to focus on their moral upbringing manners and behavior. Common courtesies Things taught in the home like yes, please and thankyou shapes colors "thank you","" yes" and" please", - common courteously and discipline- to some was like a foreign language. In public school children reared from that elk were labeled as behavioral challenged, troublemakers and problem children. They were classified as uneducable, dumped into special education or transferred to "bad schools like redirection and forgotten.

I was taught very early in my life about the value of an education from my grandfather and my mother. Their words reverberate in my mind still to this day. "You can be anything you want to be in this world as long as you get your education", my grandfather used to say. He'd even say that I could be the president of the united stated if I worked hard enough. My mother also stressed the importance of believing in yourself and your abilities. She sat me down daily and explained to me that I could do anything I put my mind to. she told me never believe that someone is better than you no matter what they might have no matter what they might say or do. She would tell me to always have your own mind-and never let others influence you to do wrong. My mother taught me how to say my bedtime prayers-how to say grace before meals and the importance of believing in god. She wasn't saved sanctified or filled with the Holy Ghost or nothing, but she was born a Christian and I guess it was her duty to pass Christian virtues on to her child. These early lessons had a profound effect on the way I viewed myself and the way I would behave towards others later in my life. These were the first teachings I would receive that would leave an impression on my mind like carvings engraved in stone dug up from the earth after many moons.

The first day of classes my mother kissed me on my cheek and said" I love you baby, "make sure you pay attention raise, your hand and participate, listen, fold your hands and be good- and no talking". My first day at school was relatively uneventful. My teacher Mrs. Sherman had asked all the students in class to stand up in class, introduce and tell the class a little something about themselves. Being that I was shy, I had seated myself in the back of the classroom to remain as unnoticeable hidden and discreet as possible, it would soon be my turn to stand up in front of a room full of what I considered to be total strangers. The thought of it made my heart pound, my underarms leaked, and my mouth ran dry. As it stood, I was very self-conscious because at my age I was the tallest boy in the first grade. My young life would become a nightmare if I made a fool of myself in front of all my new classmates by shuddering, choking up, muttering and slurring my words while all eyes were on me.

I thought, "what if they laughed". My nervousness was mounting. I felt short of breath. I was panting. If they did laugh, I would never be the same.

I chose the chair tucked strategically in the corner next to the window. All the students had introduced themselves leaving all but two students, me and a girl. For what seemed like an eternity-or I guess for me it was slow motion- the girl greeted her classmates. Her voice a smooth stiletto of sound exuded confidence and self-assurance. I wished she would talk forever so that my turn would never come. I wished that some divine providence of god would intercede to deliver me from this most uncomfortable situation. Unfortunately, my prayers would go unanswered. She was finished it was my turn all eyes were on me. I stood up on trembling legs looked out into an ocean of new faces cleared my throat and began to speak. My prayers were answer. My voice vibrated across the room like a megaphone for all to hear. It was a deep alto. "My name is Alexander Brent, "I am six years old and I live in Langston Hughes". After my initial introduction it was smooth sailing. I told of my hobbies my likes and my dislikes. It was like I couldn't shut my mouth. My mother was right when she said anything you put your mind to you would be able to achieve if only you believed. And at that moment I had my mind squarely focused on not making myself look like a damn fool.

Mrs. Sherman was a pretty good teacher, she taught us how to read, write and do arithmetic. We would go to another room for art class in the art room we painted colored and created things with clay, cardboard, Lagos or whatever our creative minds could endeavor. Social studies and science were also held in separate rooms. I was fascinated by each. Social studies gave me a mind's eye view of the places and peoples that existed in the vast outer world beyond the invisible barriers of the ghetto interior that kept most of its inhabitants trapped perpetually in an existence fuel by poverty self-hate and despair. Science explained the meaning of why things existed in the outer and inner worlds and beyond. I would directly envision these things in my mind after reading, studying or viewing their pictures on paper. It was like I was there. For me I guess it was a way to escape the boring monotony of everyday existence. As a result, I began to daydream.

I was a very bright and exceptional student to say the least. In the second grade I learned how to read at fourth

10

grade level. I was good at writing short stories and very creative artistically with my hands. Being shy or introverted didn't serve as an obstacle to disable or limit me it made me better. While others focused on the superficiality of the external world around them living in fantasy- I focused on the internal world, the world unseen by the extroverts who always looked outside of themselves - the world of mind and intellect-the world that separates the known from the unknown. At times during class lessons I would begin to daydream because my mind wasn't satisfied with the small amount of mental stimulus I was receiving from the dull drab and monotone teacher who taught lesson that I had learned before. I became the butt of jokes from my peers because I would be caught daydreaming by the teacher. On one such occasion when he decided to call on me to answer a question, he had caught me unaware lost in my dream world. My head was facing upwards towards the window. My teacher exclaimed "Alex", "Alex", "are you there", "come in Alex"! I snapped out of my dream to find all eyes on me awaiting my response to a question which I never heard. I was baffled, dumbfounded and considerably embarrassed because I had no answer and no explanation. I mustered enough strength to ask in the most forgiving tone for him to repeat the question. He stared straight at me and began to shout at the top of his lungs, "Mars to Alex come in Alex". Thus, the humiliating nickname "mars man" was born-and would cause me a considerable amount of discomfort for some time to come. Though I worked and studied hard in school it seemed that since the discovery of my daydreaming secret the teacher began to openly persecute me by teasing and embarrassing me every chance he could get. My classmates felt they had been given justification to begin teasing me also. my grades began to suffer I became withdrawn and completely antisocial. Open school night had begun. This was the period in the school year that most students dreaded the most. You could get your ass whipped for the smallest bullshit the teacher said you did. if your parents came to open school night and the teacher said your grades were suffering because of you talking in class, not paying attention, chewing gum, or not doing homework-this constituted serious grounds for immediate butt naked ass whipping on the spot in front of the teacher. To say the least this was the source of every child's ultimate fear.

My mother was a trooper- she never accepted the teacher's assessment of her child when on the many occasions he would write notes or call her personally stating to her that somehow, I had a problem. My mother always believed in me. She knew the level of work I was cable of performing. She knew my strengths as well as my weaknesses. I would always call her at work when I returned home from school to give her a personal run down of the events of the day. She knew of the harassment and the other forms of intimidation that my teacher along with my peers had subjected me to. On more than one occasion she had engaged him in a heated discussion over the phone. She openly scolded him for his often-pernicious behavior towards me - a child in whose care he was supposed to protect- not humiliate, mock, abuse and then blame for not performing up to par.

It was open school night. Today was the day that the two would finally meet. It would be a day that would change the course of events in my short and acutely tumultuous life.

It was 7:00 o'clock, my mother tired from the events of the day had just returned from working a job that promised few benefits and little rewards. For some strange reason the night was extra dark. My school looked like a forbidden castle with these two immense glowing eyes - the schools windows - but at night to a child with a vivid imagination they became the source of every hidden fear. As we approached my stomach began to dance, electric slide and butterfly all at the same time. I had wished the darkness would swallow me up so that I could never be found. My mother introduced herself greeting my teacher cordially an exchange of pleasantries masking their true intentions. My teacher had this subtle air of bourgeoisie arrogance about him that would intimidate the average parent born and raised in the confines of the ghetto. Because of his title, schooling, education and status, he believed he could snub his nose out talk and awe so called common Black folk with use of language to silence them into submission. My mother had some college education under her belt so his intimidation would not faze her at all.

"Ms. Brent it's a pleasure to meet you", said my teacher looking my mother deeply in her eye- an intimidation tactic that worked for him during numerous encounters with belligerent parents in the past." "I'm glad we finally have a chance to meet at conference". "I'm concerned about your son's progress". "As a teacher it is in my best interest as an authority and as a professional educator to assess the situation and provide you with the best analysis capable to resolve any and all dilemmas which may be endemic to the ratification of any barriers your son might be facing". This bourgeoise motherfucker pondered my mother, he doesn't know who he's fucking with; she smiled inwardly. "Yes, it is true that your position as an educator enables you to analyze the behaviors of various students in order to judge their progress as students". "But in order to foster and reinforce confidence and self-assurance in students- which is the foundation of a well-rounded student-educators being in authoritative positions must bolster the self-esteem of students not destroy it". He raised his eyebrow, silently he was impressed by her verbal acumen. "We are here to discuss your child's problem Mrs. Brent". "My ethics are not on trial here". "Mrs. Brent let me be honest with you". "Here are records of your child's work". He presented my schoolwork pointing out words and numbers that were spelled backwards." your child's work indicates that the apparent problem he faces is dyslexia". "He also has a problem listening and understanding my instructions which may also be indicative of attention deficit disorder". "We can have your child tested". "We have number programs we could provide you with that may be able to suit his needs". "If this problem is not resolved", stated my teacher "I would have to have him placed in a special education program for the learning disabled".

"Once labeled, the teacher exclaimed, he would get the special assistance needed for children with his disability".

Trying to mask his impending anger at the assertion by my mother that he was an incompetent teacher, he sat back smugly believing he had scared my mother into submission. My mother now looked through his soul with her piercing eyes-this made him inwardly nervous. "Mr. McDowell do you have your doctorate degree". He replied; Yes, I do but…" the teacher was quickly cut off in mid-sentence" do you have a degree in psychology". "No, you do not, my mother replied. "My son has passed all of your test, done all his schoolwork and homework. "If he has performed all that was expected of him academically then why are you pushing to have my child classified as learning disabled". "The only reason for his learning disabilities lies in your ineffective and harmful teaching methods". "I will continue this conversation with your superiors, if no resolution is reached then I will have this unfortunate situation resolved in court". My teacher sat dumbfounded and was unable to give an adequate response. It was a glorious day, I felt free. I would no longer feel intimidated or afraid to speak my mind, I knew I had the support of my mother.

The rest of the school year was relatively easy. I was still teased by my peers because my nickname had stuck. As for Mr. McDowell he never called on me again-and that's just the way I liked it. Other than the boring and annoying shit done in class, the most exciting part of the day was lunchtime or what we called munch time. Three o'clock was also an exciting time of the day not because it was time to go home but because it's time to see who was going to get their ass wiped and who was going to do the ass wiping.

Lunch time in school was a time when boys got to be boys. Boys got to test each other's strength by means of slap boxing arm wrestling or playing ball or any activity that required physical contact. By besting other boys through slap boxing a boy basically acquired his spot in the male hierarchy of dominance. This was very important to a young buck trying to be a Mack with the cuties.

It was like the military, you had to line up and march to the lunchroom single file; girls on one line, guys on the other. On the way down, we used to walk through the darkened stair wells and play the ass squeezing game. It went like this: you squeeze a girl's ass when her back was turned and act like you didn't do nothing, you just look straight ahead and play innocent. We would laugh to ourselves while the girl ranted, raved and cursed, threatening to whip the ass of anyone she thought to be the perpetrator. The popular cats could squeeze a girl's ass openly and not get beat down. The girl would lamely cry stop with a sly grin give them a love tap and begin to giggle and whisper amongst themselves. When we entered the lunchroom, we were seated together in rows according to our classes. Everyone ate together from grade one through six. Each table was made up of different crews. If you were in a click, in those days it was called "being down by law"-you would have to be given a street name. A street name wasn't the name that your momma gave you-your government name-a street name was a name your ghetto family relinquished upon you as an honored member of your click. Niggers in my click were named G-man, Shaz, Man, Mister, Jun, Cam, l-love, Skills, Black, and a host of other shit I don't care to mention at this time. Your street name denoted a part of your character. If you were respected by your peers you were given the name Mister, if you got all the bitches, l-love if you were a smooth player. It was 1979 the song Rapper's Delight hit the airwaves. As children we imitated the rappers. During lunchtime in our cafeteria we would try to emulate the rappers by performing nursery rhymes, we battled and tried to outdo each other to become the best rapper amongst our peers. We used to beat on the tables and kick rhymes.

My generation was referred to as the post baby boomers. Back in the days there was no such thing as drive-by shootings, brothers had to have hand skills. Those who possessed them would naturally want to test their skills on others who had similar talents. The schoolyard was the arena and at three o'clock the gladiators entered the courtyard. Everyone was trying to build a reputation, and anything could get you called out into the arena, a look, a bump, a stare, or something as inconsequential as stepping or someone's sneakers. The beefs always started during lunchtime. The cafeteria was a testing ground for warriors as well as those classified as cowards. A momma joke, a stare down, anything could result in you being called out into the arena for the three o'clock showdown. There was no backing out for if you declined a challenge you were automatically labeled a pussy and your reputation would be damaged for life. News traveled fast in the hood you would be labeled as a coward and everywhere you went you would be chased, tested, and physically assaulted by everyone. Punks were always trying to build a rep and hard rocks were always trying to protect their name. If you wanted to avoid becoming an outcast you had to fight, you had no options. Your manhood would be tested, and in the arena, you would take your place as a man or a chump. If you fought and lost, you would gain a degree of respect for standing up as a man. If you ran away or avoided the arena, your life would become a living hell, you would be bullied for life. Those who fought often became the best of friends after gaining a healthy respect for one another. They would later become running partners and create gangs, crews, and clicks that would fight, steal, rob, hustle or generally terrorize the rest of the ghetto masses. In those days pain and I became the best of friends for I was constantly tested by the hardest motherfuckers in Brownsville, because I had size.

CHAPTER 3 THE PROJECTS

The Crash Crew, The Old Gold Gang were crews that were known and had all the juice in the ghetto back in those days. To be initiated you had to be jumped in-a gang ritual which proved how tough, fearless and hard a motherfucker was. If you wanted to run with a crew of thirty motherfuckers you had to run through a gauntlet, fifteen cats on one side, fifteen cats on the other side; all with chains, sticks, fists, belts, bats and brass knuckles and shit. You had to run through the gauntlet and if you made it to the other side standing on your own two feet, you were in. I would soon learn that I could not separate myself from the confines of this sordid ghetto reality. I would have to get respect through use of hand game or be slaughtered like a sheep in a den of wolves.

Reflecting upon my past experiences I came to realize that degrees were not only gained in the halls of higher education, but they could be gained in the school of hard knocks when one mastered the code of street survival. Those who studied, listened, watched and learned participated and got promoted at each phase of the game, eventually gained Bachelors, Masters and Doctorates in the game. Those who failed their bones lined the cemeteries, their bodies wasted away in prisons, the drug dens and the alleys. I saw that school and the streets closely paralleled one another. The latter prepared you for the world of work-the former- the world of the hustler.

Days in school became routine filled with bouts of work bouts of play and life moved ever forward in its slow methodical way. During that time my grades improved, I got promoted to the next grade, I even had an opportunity to skip a grade. We moved from my grandfather's house to my aunt cookie's home. Though still in Brownsville, the area was startlingly different yet the same in many respects. We were still in the projects, there was still unbelievable levels of poverty, and many were still mental captives in prisons built without walls. Although I met many friends as well as enemies unbeknownst to me at that time there were many lessons life had in store for me that would mold me into the man that I eventually would become.

Tilden, a project complex composed of six towers, each 16 stories respectively, housed over 2000 families, approximately 30,000 residents on a block of urban estate no larger than a mile in length, two ghetto blocks in width to be sure. 265 Livonia Avenue would become my new testing ground. Here I would encounter every formidable obstacle I would need to enable me to learn how to master and control fear; fear of others who in my naïve innocence would try to manipulate, deceive and possibly destroy me. 265 was known as the "yard". To enter you had to walk up a path were 20 to 30 hard rocks playing radios slap boxing training vicious dogs rolling dice working out smoking and rolling trees were present. This generally was the scene that accompanied residence in their quest to survive the stress of living a ghetto existence.

In my aunt's house we had to live by a set of rules. My aunt cookie was and still is to this day very religious. No rap music, no speaking god's name in vain, no cursing, no nothing. All normal activities were of the devil and was considered evil. She believed that the only way to avoid hell and damnation was to lead a pious righteous and virtuous life. We believed she went to church more than the preacher did. As children, she would always encourage us to get saved, sanctified and filled with the Holy Ghost because she believed the devil was the master of this world and god the master of the next.

In Brownsville the projects were mostly crime ridden havens for poverty. Other housing developments had reputations for being the most dangerous. Seth low, Langston Hughes, Tilden and Brownsville projects lived up to their names. In Tilden outsiders could not just come into our domain unannounced. If you didn't know anyone you would get asked a series of questions upon entering the courtyard or the lobby of our building by thugs and hard rocks patrolling the perimeter. If you gave the name of an unknown punk or sucker you got automatically robbed, smacked, roughed up or chased to the train station. In my building, you had Mae Moe, Scope, Derek and his twelve brothers. These were the thug soldiers who held the fort ruling our territory with an iron hand of fear and intimidation. Strength, vigor and brutal aggression were the characteristics that prepared you for survival in Tilden Projects. You would have to learn to be a standup motherfucker under fire or prepare yourself to never leave your house for fear of being victimized.

Just as my aunt cookie was in charge of giving spiritual instructions in her home, my mother schooled me and gave my physical instructions for the streets. These codes of conduct and rules enabled me to survive and maneuver in the concrete jungles of Brownsville. There were times I used get chased home, at other times niggers tried to extort and intimidate me. After a couple of these incidents my mother sat me down and began to give me the blueprint of the streets. The first and primary rule she taught me was to never show fear. She explained that fear more than any man was your number one enemy. Fear, she said, immobilizes man. It makes a man incapable of acting, making decisions, and thinking for himself. In my mind I wondered how this related to the streets and my current situation. As I looked back at that time, I reflected on the many things my mother said and she was right. She told me everything in life requires a level of boldness and courage. Courage had a strong impact upon your will and your will determined how far you would succeed in life. She told me that fear destroys will power. She stated you not only become afraid of others, you become afraid to do things because of fear of failure. Reflecting to the lessons, mother reiterated the importance of standing up for oneself. She emphasized that no matter how ferocious your enemy appeared to be, always look them in the eye and never back down. She said backing down, running or submitting to victimization, was a symbol of cowardice and in this world a man would never gain respect by being a punk. Mother was brutally honest and direct with me as she lovingly fed me the naked truth. Even if you fight a man and lose, you would be respected because you have heart. When you fight, she said, battle with all your heart because symbolically you are at a state of war, and in the streets no rules apply. If your enemy is bigger than you, hit him with a stick, a chair, kick him in the nuts, cut him with a knife, but let him know that your there to do business-and if necessary, to kill or be killed.

She explained the philosophical aspect of ghetto survival. In the animal kingdom, the first and primary law is survival of the fittest. This natural law applied to the law of natural selection.

This law states that only the strongest male in any group- be it animal bird fish or man- can reproduce with female members of their kind only if they prove they can protect females and their offspring from other competing males. She explained that in the animal kingdom the female made her choice of mate by breeding with the strongest of the competing males. This ensured that strong children would be produced. If a male animal was thought to be weak the female would test his prowess by attacking him. If he fled in fright, he would never gain the privilege of reproducing offspring- and character flaws such as cowardice would successfully be eliminated from that animals' biological gene pool. My mother explained to me how the same applies to human beings although we are on a higher level of development.

She explained the sociological aspect about fear and courage and its impact on men in the ghetto. She explained to me that men always competed in sports as well as on the battlefield of life to best each other; and to those who were winners in these competitions they were given honors, titles and first pick of the choice's females. Those who proved themselves became leaders to those who were naturally weaker. Case in point, she bluntly stated to me that no woman wants a punk ass man. Therefore, the fly girls only fuck with the hard rocks, players, hustlers, ballers and popular guys because a woman wants to know she has a man with clout, character and strength to protect her name and her fame. A woman had a sense of pride knowing that she was protected. The lessons my mother taught me were drilled into my psyche. I now understood the reason young men fought so hard to get a reputation and keep it. Why the prisons and cemeteries were filled with so many of them who died to hold on to their status in a land were a man with a name was king. As a child I pondered these concepts stating that I would apply them to my life in order to improve my position in the Ghetto hierarchy. Coincidentally I would get to test the soundness of this newfound philosophy sooner than I had anticipated. Ma Moe was a known thug and hard rock. I knew the time was fast approaching when he would test my manhood as he had tested others before me. I would have to be ready mentally and physically. We lived in the same building on the same floor. I was on the east side of the building; he was on the west side. On occasions we would happen to run into each other in the hallway. At times he would try to intimidate me by staring me down. Back in the days if you stared at a man more than 10 seconds that was grounds for a beat down. The tension between me and Mae-Mo was thick. Each time we crossed paths the intimidation grew bolder. He began to utter comments under his breath about fucking me up. He laughed and mocked me when he was amongst his friends. I remembered the instructions I received from my mother. I had butterflies in my stomach, this was the fear my mother tried to prepare me to master in the face difficulties. It would be up to me to handle this situation on my own.

Mother knew me well, she noticed that something was wrong because I seemed preoccupied for a couple of weeks. I guess at times she knew me better than I knew myself. Indeed, there were many issues facing me at that time. I was young black and living in a hell not of my making. I was trapped and had to use the cunning of a fox to escape my captors in a cage where the bars were invisible. By nature, I wasn't a predator like those I encountered on the streets of Brownsville who were heavily muscled, shirtless, and ready to beat murder and maim for the smallest infraction. I was a lamb, a man of peace, but I had to prepare myself to walk through the valley of the shadow of death. This night I was prepared to be the black sheep and do whatever was necessary to defend myself. It was dinner time, my mother called me to the dinner table. She noticed something was wrong, my countenance gave it away. Boy what's wrong with you, she asked. I shook my head and she made no further inquiry. Listen Ale I need you to run to the store and get me some rice. Immediately my heart began beating furiously, and my stomach began to feel fucked up. With a strained and shaky voice, I answered in the affirmative. "Boy come get this money and stop acting stupid," she said motioning to me. Everything seemed to move in slow motion at that moment. It was if my legs were frozen. My mother was right about fear t immobilizing a man. I had no doubt that the moment I stepped out of that door into the night I would encounter the source of my fear. I knew I would eventually have to face my fears, so I threw caution into the wind and said fuck it. I put on my coat and walked out the door. At night, the projects seemed unquestionably menacing to the uninitiated. The hallways were a mess of graffiti-littered with cigar tobacco, stained with piss and on occasion shit. It was a nightmarish world where the faint of heart need not travel. As I proceeded out the door the hallway the lights were dim and flickering from years of neglect. I heard the audible sounds of radios whispering from the stairwell and the crackle of gunfire in the distance. I paced myself and began to move out on my journey. The sounds of crying babies and lovers quarreling resounded through my ears. I crept silently towards the stairwell consciously avoiding the elevator. As I neared the door and began to open it, I noticed a shadowy figure briskly moving in the dank stairwell. As the door slowly opened it was as if I was entering a house of horrors and had come face to face with my greatest fear. It was Mae Mo; he was by himself-fortune smiled on me. If this was the time for us to knuckle up, it would be one on one, no jumping no double or triple teaming. This would be a battle to the finish and only one of us would come out on top. He stared through me and spoke. Big man what you got for me, he said. I don't have nothing for you, I retorted. An icy fear shot through my body as I braced for the inevitable. Where you going? I need some dough kid- all I find all I keep motherfucker. He began to tap my pants pockets probing for money and change. I moved backward through the stairwell door facing Mae Mo as he moved forward trying to intimate me. I moved into the narrow confines of the hallway. Mae Mo sensing that I would be an easy victim rushed towards me and dug his hand into my pockets. My strategy was to lull him into a false sense of confidence and then strike. He tried to strong arm me throwing me up against the wall. I gave up no resistance. I laughed on the inside because I was about to fuck this nigga up for testing my manhood. Mae Mo had his forearm pressed on my chest digging his hands into my pockets then I exploded. I screamed in anger and struck him with the palm of my hand, his head flew backwards into the hard cement wall. Dazed shocked and confused he screamed as I wailed on his body and head with crushing lefts and rights. He cowered crumbling into a fetal position to cover himself from the volley of blows, I rained down upon him. At that moment I felt something I had never experienced before, a sense of control.

My body was hot, adrenaline coursed through my veins, I felt virile. This is what it felt like to be a predator-I reasoned. I lost all sense of time as I rained blows on Mamo for the years of anguish he subjected me to. I struck a blow for all the years of living in fear, the years of regret for not striking back against those who had wrong me without cause. I fought like an enraged animal punching kicking and stomping him. The commotion alerted the neighbors like flies attracted to shit. My mother rushed into the mist of our flailing bodies attempting to separate us. She stopped nodding her head in silent approval as she watched me fight to gain respect, redemption and recognition as a man. She had seen his type before; he was a bully a predator and a criminal in training. This would be a lesson that he would learn, a painful lesson. That day I had gained the respect of my peers, news spread fast that I was not to be fucked with. I could have used the opportunity to gain a reputation but that was not my motivation, I just wanted to be left alone. I wanted to live my life in peace and security free from fear and intimidation. From that day on others approached me as a man. They interacted with me from a position of respect.

Funny how fate can change the worst situation for the better. Me and Mae Mo instead of becoming die-hard enemies became the best of friends.

CHAPTER 4 MY FATHER

Life flowed, thugs fought, some were killed, others were locked up, but the streets remained the same. Me and my mother stayed with my Auntie Cookie for over four years, then my stepfather returned home from jail and everything changed. His name was Leon, in the streets he was known as Junior. My mother had known Junior since she was nine years old. He was older and used to protect her from unwanted advances of other men. My mother was fascinated by him, she considered him a man's man. He was street wise, knew how to handle himself and was respected in the hood. He wore Stacy Adam shoes, Fedora Hat's and long trench coats. He was the quintessential smooth player and a thug. His hand and knife game gave him fame. When cats heard his name, they looked over their shoulders in fear. He was one of those short, stocky, black, built, broad nosed cats with fierce eyes and a trigger temper. He was a lady's man and a hustler, but to my mother he was her man. He and my mother grew up together, Junior was her first love. She rebelled against my Grandmother and Grandfather to be with him. She ran away with him to Staten Island when our grandfather forbade her to see him anymore. My mother was so in love with Junior I think she would have given a pint of her own blood to be with him. He introduced my mother to the 'in crowd', she was a made chick, she was Leon's girl and he introduced her to his world. She knew the players, the ballers, hustlers and the thieves. He always asked my mother to promise him that she wouldn't get knocked up by no other man when he got locked up. Every time he came home, he tried vigorously to get her pregnant, but was unsuccessful. Junior's partner in crime was a cat he met upstate named BoDee. He and BoDee used to play ball and gangbang upstate. Junior admired BoDee because his hand skills were strong. He used to knock out two and three niggas at a time during gang fights. He was feared by many because of his volatile temper and violent reputation. BoDee came home before Leon and vowed he would lookout for my mother while he was locked down and he stuck to his promise. When BoDee returned home he hooked up with my Aunt Cookie, they were pen pals while he was incarcerated.

Junior remained incarcerated for four years while BoDee ran the streets. He had later introduced my mother to his brother Sunny. The chemistry between the two were immediate and sparked into a heated romance. My mother had gotten pregnant and later I was born. BoDee followed suit, shortly thereafter he impregnated my aunt who bore his only son whose name was DJ. Both sisters carried the seed of two brothers in their wombs. However, the seed of betrayal was planted in the mind of my mother who feared the repercussion of her actions. Had Junior known the child he would call his own was in fact another man's, she feared he might kill Sunny to protect his rep. A dark cloud loomed over my mother as she contemplated the karmic consequences that disloyalty, infidelity and broken oaths could bring. She would give Junior what he so earnestly desired but would never reveal the deep dark secret that the child she bore was not his. After returning home from jail my Mother and Junior later got married. He worked odd jobs but was never able to find gainful employment sufficient to support his family. On the other hand, my mother had a steady job with the City of New York, she had graduated from high school, was making good money, attended college at night and was capable of supporting herself independently. Feeling as though he was losing authority in his household, Junior began to drink, get high and hang out. That's when the beatings and the physical abuse began. My mother endured and suffered violence at his hand yet continued to keep a brave face in the face of all the abuse. I was severely affected by the chaos that permeated my household. On many occasions' Junior used to beat my mother bloody for the smallest infraction. Insecurity, pride and ego were an explosive mix in the hands of a man with misogynist, male chauvinist and sociopathic tendencies. Violence in his hands was used as a tool to exact control and authority over my mother who he felt was trying to emasculate him and usurp his authority as head of the household. She had to report where she was, who she had spoken with, what time she would return home, who her friends where and how much money she had made when she was paid. If mother ever protested or raised her voice in any way regarding his unreasonable request, she ran the risk of being assaulted. Sometimes the abuse occurred in my mist. I would hear the violent rumbling, rambling, cursing, crashing and screaming sounds of fierce struggle as I lay frozen in my bed during the night.

I recalled our lessons on fear and pondered was it to be used on one's family. It was said that fear was employed to intimidate one's enemies and courage was the only means to combat it. But the irony was my Mother was sleeping with the enemy and knew not where to turn. She was confused and suffered a multitude of emotions from love to fear, anxiety to hatred. She wanted to leave but over time she began to lose the will to resist. Junior had a psychological effect on her that she could not break free of. I was confused, how could my father profess to love my mother on the one hand but hurt and brutalize her on the other. I felt defenseless, there was nothing I could do. I hated him; I prayed every night for God to take his miserable life. But justice has a way of moving slower than the hands of clock but move it did. My prayers were answered swiftly like monsoon rains released upon sun scorched grasslands. The animosity between my mother and Junior continued to intensify to the point where life with him became unbearable. I would never forget the situation that led to that explosive day. It all happened when I was coming home from school. I was on the bus; it was packed to the rafters during the evening rush. People of every description comingled in the confines of this tightly packed sardine can. It was particularly hot that day and I drifted in and out of consciousness like a dope fiend on heroin. I was awakened by a dab of spit that had trickled down my lip like a spider's web. Rubbing my face with the rough side of my jacket sleeve I focused my eyes and realized that I was in unfamiliar territory. I panicked pulled the cord and exited the bus darting off into the night. I began to walk in the opposite direction which I came. At that time I noticed that I didn't have my schoolbooks. I trembled thinking about the ass wiping that awaited me when I got home. Fear gripped me in its iron like jaws, I felt like my heart it was ready to explode.

I finally reached home and slithered like a snake towards my bedroom. My stepfather sat wide legged across the sofa watching television. He was visibly drunk, his eyes were red, he nursed his wine bottle in his left hand while his right hand rested on his crotch. In a loud guttural voice he barked, "nigga were the fuck you been". I froze in my tracks and dared not move for fear of what might transpire. Mother had not yet come from work and I was defenseless and alone. My stepfather had a way of striking terror into the hearts of his enemies through his gaze, his body language had the earmarks of a natural born predator. He walked towards me and barked, "I said were the fuck you been". Tears began to flow freely down my cheeks, my body trembled. I, struggled for words but before I could speak my words were cut short as he viscously slapped me across my face. I saw stars, the room was spinning. My stepfather had hands thick, hard, black and calloused. After slapping the shit out of me, I was automatically sent to my room. As I lay staring at the ceiling in the narrow confines of my room the darkness began to close in on me. I lay shocked and bewildered, tears of anguish flowed freely like droplets of blood from my psychological wounds. Then suddenly I heard the rustling of keys, mother was home. I feared for her safety. My heart filled with dread. What would he say? How would he approach her? I placed my ears against the wall and struggled to hear what was occurring in the living room.

My heart began to race the adrenaline flowed through my veins. My body tensed as the murmurs became louder. I could barely move each movement caused my body to crack like a dead man with rigor mortis. My breathing was shallow my mouth was dry, I crept slowly towards the door, my pace

33

was a measured painful exercise of my will. I approached the door resting my head against its cool wood paneling placing my ear in a position to eavesdrop. "Your fucking son lost his bookbag", said my father as I listen intently on the door. "Junior could you at least let me get myself together so I can start cooking dinner then we could address this situation", cried my mother. "The problem is you always treating that boy like a pussy". "If he does something wrong you always taking up for him, he needs to stand on his own two feet like a man and be more responsible". My mother responded. "Every time he does something wrong he becomes my son, but when he does something right you don't even acknowledge or reward him, you're his father too and you're not showing him how to be a man". She cut a cord deep into my father soul. "Are you trying to say I'm not a man Joe?" "That's my goddamned son and I will raise him as I damn well please". The argument began to escalate and became heated. My palms were sweaty yet my hands were ice cold. I wished to God that I was a giant so I could burst from my room and beat Junior to a pulp. But I was small, frail, powerless and immersed in a nightmare in which there was no escape. I was scared to breath for fear I could be heard. The argument became fierce. I crouched in a fetal position as I laid in the darkness.

The reality hit me, my mother and father were involved in a domestic dispute the likes of which I had never seen. The crescendo of chaos began its tumultuous ascension as their battle intensified into a war. I clamored in my bed clenching my sheets tightly around my body praying the horror would cease, yet the battle peaked. Sounds of screaming and struggle could be heard accompanied by muffled cries. I trembled transfixed like a soldier shell shocked from the insanity of war. As quickly as the battle began it subsided, not a sound could be heard. Immediately my imagination ran wild with vision of my mother lying face down in her own blood. Would I be next? Would I die clenching and clawing at the hands of an undefeatable enemy? I found myself praying again to god for deliverance at the last moments of what I felt were the closing minutes of my life. I feared the hellfire that my aunt cookie so often lectured us on.

The end was not as close as I had envisioned, it was the beginning of what would prove to be my own personal hell. I heard faint footsteps in the distance. I gasped for air, my heart skipped a beat, my hair stood on end, as I struggled to control my bowels. I gazed toward the door. The door flung open; my heart almost exploded from fear. My father bleeding from the scratches inflicted during their fight sat next to me in the bed, his dead weight sinking deep into the mattress. He sat next to me and began to explain, but I was numb with fear, his words were muffled as I could only hear the beating of my heart. His words bounced off me like bullets hitting a Kevlar vest. He continued to stress his points on deaf ears. My heart and mind were numb to his pointless philosophical explanation on the nature of control. I was seething with naked hatred and fear two emotions too volatile to express with words. At that point I was looking forward into space neither acknowledging his words or his gestures. Desperation in his eyes, he peered around the room in search of something. He looked toward the window but there was no fire escape. My body stiffened, perhaps he wanted to throw me to my death, or perhaps he was looking for an alternate route of escape. Opening the window, he peered four flights down into the alleyway.

Looking quickly towards me he grabbed me by my arm. At that moment there was heavy rattling on the door in the living room. My father scooped me up carrying me in a vise like grip and ran towards the kitchen area. Rustling through the drawers he grabbed a 12-inch kitchen knife, the living room door burst open, I was flung off the floor by my father, and placed in a choke hold. Amidst the chaotic confusion I felt the cold steel of a blade pressed against my jugular. The police had arrived. Apparently, my mother had alerted them after fleeing the apartment. Two Irish men six feet tall, two hundred pounds apiece entered our home. They had seen it all before. The typical angry unemployed negro distraught due to fear of losing authority in his home who now lashed out using the only means available to balance the playing field-brute force. They approached him with caution and tried to reason with him. However, they were startled back to reality when my father began screaming incoherently. "This is my son…mine, and no white man going to tell me how to raise him," my father said. As the situation intensified the police used precaution before approaching my father. They spoke very softly in order to diffuse the rising tension. Sir I need you to calm down, said the officer. Moving closer, the police gestured with their hands facing palm down. They continued to use reverse psychology to deescalate the situation. Approaching slowly the police officer gestured with his hands. "Guy, I understand what you're going through, I'm married too", said the officer speaking candidly. "Sometimes my wife gets on my last nerve too". The officer pulled out a pack of cigarettes and offered a stogie to my father. My father took the cigarette reluctantly all the while looking both the officers deeply in their eyes. "You all must think I'm stupid, don't con me man." He tightened his grip on me and continued to hold the knife against my throat.

Listen I'm not going to bullshit you guy your placing yourself, your old lady and your kid in a compromising position. You're not helping them my friend; you're hurting them more than anything else…. Is it worth it? "If you drop the knife, we can end this standoff peacefully". "The choice is yours guy. " The officer raised his shoulders and sighed. Holding the blade my father seemed to be lost in deep thought. At that moment my father was filled with deep regret and he dropped the knife and let me go. I ran in to my mother's arms. I'll never forget the look my mother gave June before he was led out in handcuffs. If looks could kill Junior would have been buried in an unmarked grave with a bottle of his own piss to drink. As I pondered the events of that day, I believe that was the beginning of the end for their relationship. My mother remained with him for quite some time after the incident, but she was disconnected mentally, emotionally, and spiritually. Towards the end of their relationship she just went through the motions until they finally got a divorce.

CHAPTER 5 ON THE MOVE

Mother remained single, for a while it was just me and her. We moved from the outskirts of Bedford Stuyvesant into the interior, the part of the Bed-Stuy known in those days as Do or Die. That's the part where you had your OG's, hard rocks and thugs. You were bound to be tested if you wasnt known, but Bed-Stuy couldn't fuck with Brownsville. We used to call Bed-Stuy the country. We moved to Macon St. Ours was a tree lined block full of post-World War II brown stones, some were dilapidated. These were the brownstones that were occupied by renters. Their owners were mostly slum lords or whites who fled the ghetto to the suburbs when blacks began to enter the neighborhood in mass during the early 60's. They no longer lived in the area and only gave a fuck about rent money.

Me and my mother lived in a two-bedroom apartment on the third floor. The apartment, a moderate size held a new beginning for us. Because mother was a nine to five working woman, I didn't relish the thought of becoming a latchkey kid. I was still young, a momma's boy to coin the phrase correctly. Mother was the center of my universe. I revolved around her. My connection to her was like the earth to sun. She was the source of my life. She sheltered me, gave me food, and put clothes on my back. Without her I would have withered like a plant in a dark closet. Every day after school I would call mother at work to relay the news of the day and get help with my homework. That was my way of keeping our lines of communication open. Mother began giving me allowance. It was a moderate price; about five dollars every Friday. It couldn't buy a car or get a brother fly but it was a nice piece of change. It was 1982, five dollars was the equivalent of at least 25 dollars today-believe me I was very grateful. Even though I got my palms greased at the end of the week, that dough didn't come easy. I had to work hard; mother gave me a list of chores to perform. I had to wash the dishes, take out the garbage, clean the living room, the bedroom, the kitchen and the bathroom. Suffice it to say I learned the meaning of work ethic and responsibility. At last it seemed I was happy. My life had order. My routine provided meaning to what I felt was an insignificant existence. After the turmoil of those previous years me and my mother experienced, I felt at peace being alone. I had a lot of time to sort out my feelings. Unbeknownst to me I still suffered the psychological wounds inflicted by my stepfather. I was going through a stage in my life when I had an aversion to Black men. After a day of school returning home doing chores and homework I looked forward to my mother's return from work. Mom used to bring goodies home. My favorite was snickers, in second place was chunky, in third place was Kit Kat. In order to stave away the boredom of latchkey living I also loved to play with toys and read comic books. When I brought home good grades my mother used to surprise me and bring home Stars Wars action figures, I had all the gadgets guns backpacks laser hooks, the works.

Comic books also served the purpose of keeping me occupied during the evenings after I returned home. My mother brought me all the comics of my choosing. There was Conan the barbarian, kull the conqueror, spider man, x-men, the justice league, you name it I had it. I had accumulated quite a vast collection. Comic books provided a means of escape that took away the pain of everyday living. During my lonely evenings of solitude my mind wondered into the dream realm. I envisioned myself as a conquering warrior overcoming my enemies or a powerful superhero who saved the world getting the girl in the end. I was trying to understand the world that I was in. The boredom was depressing. I dug into the creative genius inside of me and begin to create toys with my hands. I also began to draw miniature comic strips. I was alone I had no friends in the neighborhood so I didn't really go outside often. When I dared ventured outside there was a makeshift park-the only park in the area-the park had no name it was lodged between to brownstone buildings. It had a monkey bars a miniature wooden fort with a sliding board it was substandard but it had to do. I played with the neighborhood kids on the block. In our mini park we played tag, roundup, steal the bacon, kick the can, skelly, and a host of other games we just made as we went along. Though I played along with the bunch I never felt that I belonged to a part of a group-I always felt alone. I guess I was a loner of sorts unable to form close bonds with others. As I reflect I think it had something to do with my mother's relationship to my stepfather that created in me a hatred and aversion for adults as well as adolescent males. As a latch key kid, I began to love being to myself. The silence of the afternoon was golden as compared to the utter chaos of the morning. Commuting to school, the disorder, confusion that awaited me in the public school system with its indifferent teachers unruly students, the fights, the harassment the name calling those served as factors for me cherishing the isolation of being alone, because in my world I was king.

Then an event transpired in my life that would test the boundaries of my seemingly enclosed reality shaking my otherwise delicate world to its very foundations. The worst fear of all to a child living in a single parent headed household is to lose one's parent to death or abandonment. I was no different, better yet I was more paranoid than most to say the least. One day after arriving from school, doing my chores and finishing my homework, I relaxed watched a little television and fell into my daily routine. My mother was a very ordered woman. She got up at 7:30am woke me up fixed breakfast took a shower made sure I had any and all available necessities I needed for the day then she departed at 8:15 or 8:30 to arrive to work at about 9:00. Just as the sun rising and setting gave one and indication of the time of day, my mother's daily routine gave me a sense of time and order. I had watched the 'facts of life' a television show that came on channel five after 'different strokes' had gone off. It was 6:00 o'clock mother had never come home at that time and I didn't receive any phone calls from her indicating that she would be late, or she would make a stop before arriving. I began to reason, maybe the trains broke down, maybe she didn't have money for a phone call, or all the phones might be fucked up-cause in my neighborhood motherfuckers was always 'jimmying' the phones in order to get the money out the coin slot or trying to get free calls so most of the phones always remained in a state of disrepair, in other words the was fucked up. 6:30, 7:00 o'clock 7:00 o'clock 7:30 as time moved forward my fear intensified. I waited by the phone, no phone call. I looked out the window no mommy. It was nighttime the clock was fast approaching 8:00 o'clock. My stomach began to bubble and churn. Fear has a way of making it do that sometimes. My mind began to get the best of me. I envisioned my mother behind a dumpster dead in some strange place. I envisioned her calling out for me to help her while her captors tormented her ruthlessly. My mind always had the ability to view all my thoughts in high definition and at times was my worst enemy. It was fast approaching 8:25pm my mother had never been off schedule. I had to be strong and not lose my cool, I had to think and stay in control. 8:30: a lump began to well up in my throat all reason went out the fucking window and I began to heavily sob crying like a fucking baby, because in my mind I thought my mother was dead. After my initial sense of fear subsided, I got mad as hell and sprang into action. It was 8:45 I threw on my tee shirt, and a pair of pants, put knives into my pocket, and I was out. I took to the streets; every mother fucker was my potential enemy. Every tugged-out nigger I saw I was 'ice grilling' the shit out of them; I broke the two-minute rule and was staring 'cats' in their eyes daring them to fuck with me. As far as I knew I was all alone in the world, because I truly believed that my mother would never return, so basically, I just didn't give a fuck. You know that kind of anger that you feel that's so intense you start crying and be ready to fight anybody, even the mother fucking devil, that's the anger I had towards the world that day. I continued to search the neighborhood scouring all the corner stores and seedy shady hangouts throughout my neighborhood. My body was tense as hell, I was numb, I hardly felt like I was breathing. My eyes bloodshot from crying earlier, had become swollen. I doubled back and checked all the spots I had previously searched. A sense of defeat descended into my soul as I felt hopelessly lost in a state of depression. It became a struggle just walking- each step was labored. Just then, out the corner of my eye I spotted someone who distinctly resembled- in posture, gait, and walk-my mother. As she moved closer; her silhouette being uncloaked by the darkness of the ghetto, she appeared as if by magic, it was my mother. She was warm I recognized her scent like a lost mare reunited with its mother. Running towards her, I nearly collapsed crumbling into her arms in a damn near fetal position. All my built-up anxiety exploded into a flood of emotion. I sobbed uncontrollably looking like a bitch with too much make-up on. In a mixture of fear, rage, disbelief, and happiness I screamed, "Where were you", demanding to know all the details in order to alleviate those fears which permeated my mind. My mother had no idea what ordeal I had suffered and looked at me incredulously like I was a damn fool. "Boy what the hell is wrong with you", she demanded. "Why the hell are you outside this time of night", she looked me up and down checking to see if I was ok. Grabbing me she drew back surprised by the assortment of weaponry I held. "Have you lost your natural mind", she exclaimed- the fear etched on her face beginning to mount?

"Mom I thought I lost you". My voice was barely audible amidst the stuttering, choked up, sound resounding from my voice, as well as the lump I had in my throat. My mother looked at me with both compassion, and love. In that moment she began to realize the importance of her position, and the strength the bond between mother and child held that would compel a child of my age to search the streets in a frantic effort to locate, protect, or kill-any real or imagined foe that threatened the sanctity of our bond. Quickly taking me under her wing my mother smiled kissing my cheek, I immediately relaxed feeling a sense of comfort and protection in her gesture. She began to explain, "baby I just stopped off to get a few groceries for dinner, that's all, nothing to worry, although it looks as though you may have had other ideas", she exclaimed. We walked down the dark foreboding streets. The sidewalks cracked and dilapidated gave into the hand of nature growing weeds and various fauna through its cement armor in a natural effort beautify what had been made ugly. As we strolled all the while I thought what a fool I was. I was embarrassed because I gave in to the fear letting it direct my thoughts. I was no longer in control. My mother had schooled me on the various ways fear paralyses some, or makes others act in foolish and heinously ways. I had failed to enact what I had learned philosophically as a child I and I felt as though I had failed myself. When I look back and reminisce, I was on a mission. But I learned a very insightful lesson that day. I learned that mastery involves trial and error. Rome wasn't built in a day, as they say, so I knew that there would be many other situations and chances for me to achieve mastery over the fear. By bringing it under control I would aspire to maturity and manhood. Me and ma-dukes chilled in Bed-Stuy for a minute-about two and a half more years. During that time my mother put in applications for housing, it was just cheaper than private housing, and in the projects, you didn't have to pay light, gas, or electric, and the rent was relatively less expensive, all you might have to put up with was niggas, and crime, that's about all.

CHAPTER 6 RETURN TO THE VILLE

My mother was finally called off the waiting list for housing, and we were on our way back to the Brownsville. It was home, all our family was there, and I didn't have to commute back and forth every day. All I had to do was to walk a couple of blocks down. We returned to Brownsville that same year. I can't say that I missed the Bedstuy, I didn't. Coming home gave me a new appreciation for all that I had left behind. I guess I was just ghetto and the ghetto was a part of me, because I was real to the core. The smell of refer in the lobby, broken glass, piss in the elevator, and shit on the stairs, gave me a warm feeling of comfort, I knew I had returned to the land of my birth. I know that probably sounds kind of bugged out but once from Brownsville you remain a Brownsville nigga to the day you die. We returned that year we moved into Vandyke houses. Vandyke was a massive housing complex that spanned an area one mile long by one-mile square. In width it spanned from Sutter Avenue, to Livonia Avenue, separated by an artificial boundary-the elevated number 2 and 3 subway lines. We moved to 414 Sutter Avenue, or the 9 building as I called it. We lived on the eleventh floor. My window overlooked Seth low houses, and the methadone clinic. It was the beginning of the eighties. I was about thirteen years old. The Hip Hop era was in full swing. Cats were wearing Bill Blass suits, Playboy shoes, fresh Lee Denim jeans, name belts, Puma Suits, sneakers with the fat shoelaces, Gazelles, and sporting big boom boxes. You had various crews and clicks sprouting up around the neighborhood. These crews and clicks were loosely affiliated groups of young men who hung out, played dice, smoked weed, and hash, robed hustled and stole for cash. This element lied throughout the community; it was this element that my mother strove to keep me away from. Mom made sure I always had all the latest toys and action figures to keep me occupied. She also bought me comic books to peak my interest because most of my waking hours were spent sheltered within the confines of my home. But it was hard to separate me from the natural pull of the ghetto's environment, with all its vices. These cats around me were into a lot of shit; mainly sticking up chumps for cheese and throwing dice to make rice. Drug dealing wouldn't become the mainstay of the ghetto economy until the mid-eighties during the 'ghetto wars'-more on that later. I was fascinated by the mystique thugs and players in my neighborhood possessed. Careful to obey the rules of ghetto etiquette I made sure I didn't eye a motherfucker down, but I peeped how they carried themselves in front of women and other men.

I peeped the latest styles of gear and sneaker wear, careful to note every detail for proper imitation. Back in the day's thugs were called hard rocks. In the eighties they began calling themselves B-Boys. And the fly chicks and the down bitches were called B-girls. My mother tried her best to impress upon me the importance of not being a follower-but a leader. She cited numerous examples of followers who were caught up in other people's bullshit. She told of those who had been killed for running with the in-crowd, or those in the wrong place at the wrong time, how they were locked up as accessories to crimes they did not commit. She stressed the importance of using sound judgment, and common sense, when choosing the choice of people, you choose to deal with. She always told me to have your own mind. She stated that those who were followers dressed like everyone else, did what everyone else did; they had no self-identity. It was these types of people who were in gangs, who were on drugs, in the graveyards and the penitentiary because they searched for their identity in the streets, they tried to find their identity through other people. She even got biblical on me stating that there would be many who would travel down the broad path leading to destruction, but very few would be worthy to travel down the narrow path of life. I listened, I shook my head, I said yes mam, all right, mmm-hmm, ok, I will, I will, true, true, but everything she said to me that day went in one ear and came out the other. She was dropping mad science on me, she blessed me with mad jewels continuing to build and instruct me, but my young mind wasn't ready for that level of understanding. Most of the things she said went right over my head. Quiet as kept, I thought my peers-the players b-boys, b-girls, hustler and stick up kids were mad cool. I looked up to the known niggas and silently wished I had the finesse savvy and shrewdness these cats possessed. I was a man on the outside looking in, wishing to be part of the in crowd.

My mother probably already knew my feelings and insecurities – she was intuitive that way-that is why she schooled me so vigorously when she felt that I was getting mentally weak and becoming more susceptible to the lure of the ghetto. She had already traveled the road I now trotted, and she recognized the obstacles, the pitfalls, and the traps that I had to deal with on my road to manhood. She probably knew that I wouldn't listen, but once she had spoken, her words would remain deeply embedded in my mind waiting to be fertilized by the numerous test and situations life had to offer. She always told me that it was experience that taught man life's unwritten lessons. She used to say, boy just wait to you get my age, you'll see, she said" and then you'll come back and thank me, because you'll know that everything, I told you was true. But of course, in my mind I thought she was just an old fashion woman telling me some shit that didn't apply to my life's circumstances, but in the long run I would find out that she was right, and in the long run, I would see.

We were the new heads in my building, and I was fresh meat to niggas who already came through the meat grinder and had been 'seasoned' and prepared for ghetto life. Niggas on the street as well as jails have a way of 'sizing' a nigga up assessing whether he hard or pussy. I already knew the game because quiet as kept I was already seasoned born and raised in the belly of the ghetto since birth and raised in the fire-but niggas don't know, so to them I still had to be tested. I'm not conceited or anything, but I was taught the best way to survive in the ghetto was always to keep it moving. I was taught to be courteous and say what's up but I was told to never let people know too much about you, and how you rolling, cause in reality they're not trying to be friendly, they're just sizing you up, like a fox sizes up chickens in a hen house-in the end he'll try to swallow you up. So, I just used to move back and forth from school, to home, from home to school. Cats used to glare at me hard trying to figure out who I was. It was up to them to make themselves known, because those thought to be too friendly were thought to be weak and open to be preyed upon.

I remember the first day I was approached in my building by this cat named kyki. Kyki was charcoal black rugged stone face nigga with a hawk nose who had respect on the north side of Vandyke projects cause he used to run with a crew of stick up kids. I was on my way from school and I was walking through the courtyard; which was usually packed in the winter with thirty or more mother fuckers, hooded down, in the summer, with chicken heads, hoochie mommas, and thugs who were swelled up from pumping iron last winter. It was spring so the coats were slowly coming off and Black men and women had to show what they were made of. The winter was over, and women were coming out of hibernation. You could tell the girls who stayed in the house eating cornbread and grits because they were thick at the hips. Chicks sat on benches smoking New Ports with multicolored head rags. Those who were pregnant last winter dropped their loads and sported post pregnancy bodies, some wore they hair combed straight back with the heels of their feet sticking out their shoes, while others smiled displaying mouths full of gold teeth and ears elongated by heavy door knocker earrings. As I passed through this gauntlet of ghetto humanity that assembled themselves strategically on benches which peppered the periphery of the front of my ghetto residency, I was filled with a mixture of awe as well as revulsion. Who was I to judge them, I pondered, they reflected me, and I reflected them? As I passed through, thirteen cats were engaged in a dice game in front of the building. These cats were stone cold

49

hustlers, everyone in that circle was fly. They all had on Sergio Tacchini suits, Fila's sneakers and jewelry. They sported BVD nylon tank tops, some wore Cazal's with frames and without. They sported two finger and four fingered gold rings, while others wore initial rings on each of their fingers. Others wore Adidas with no shoelaces adorning fresh nylon stocking caps concealing a head full of jail waves. They played dice- for what I perceived as big money back in those days. Niggas had tens, twenties, five, and one-dollar bills crumpled in their hands; and a pile of neatly stacked dollar bills laying in the middle of them as bank. It looked like at least five hundred dollars.

Playing dice was a uniquely African American ritual for black males in the ghetto. It established you as a young player and an up and coming baller. There are what you call secular skills, those you employ in the business world, and then there are skills you acquire in the ghetto, playing dice, spades, learning how to hustle and how to play basketball. If you didn't acquire either of these skills, you would never be considered a real nigga, and would always be relegated to the status of a square ass chump. In the Ghetto you learned and strived to become the best at acquiring and maintaining some level of street knowledge. Those who were nice at rolling dice and swift with card gift or had the ability to brake motherfucker's pockets often earned names like C-low, Ace, Deuce or Tray. In the ghetto those who mastered games of chance had to have quick reflexes, fast hands, and an agile mind; somewhat like a boxer. Those with game had to know how to evade con men and stickup kids so they had to have quick eyes. Nigga's with game also had to have technique. Some gamers were like Tyson some like Jordan and some were like Allen Iverson-most of the time they became the most valuable players in the game and got promoted to coaches- which was defined in ghetto terms as the ballers and shot callers. Some gamers retired and went legit flipping the cream to acquire the American Dream. Many brought properties and acquired businesses, these were a rarity, and they got the title of supreme OG's. But most hustled on an amateur level, at best they could wish to become an apprentice to a real live nigga in order to peek true game. Most niggas were great imitators, as children they peeped OG's styles and emulated them as much as possible. It was the only male role model most understood in a community were single motherhood was the norm. Players used technique when playing C-Low, it required attitude, it required poise. Every roller displayed a certain kind of bravado when they rolled. Veterans in the game automatically knew what was coming out they hand by the way they shook the dice, the way they positioned their hands and the pivot of their bodies and the way their hand extended when rolling their dice. They could just read you like a book if you kept your hand open.

It was humid that day. Cats were in front of my building chucking dice trying to hit sixes so they could buy jewels, cop liquor and chill with their shorties flashing cash in front of the eyes of the envious. Brothers sported flattops, freshly faded Caesar's and huddled in unison as they talked amongst themselves in the indecipherable lingo of the ghetto. C-low, cried a red eyed dark-skinned brother with a jail scar extending from his cheek ending at nape of his neck. He quickly reached down and snatched up all the cash that lay neatly piled in a heap and added it to the knot roll he already had in his pocket. He snatched up the dice and swaggered back to corner. Sweat trickled from his brow as he focused intently on the pot of cash as if in a trance. He raised his hand, blew on the dice and shook them vigorously. Yall ready to get your pockets broke, I'm about take all yall money. Staring unflinchingly, he continued shaking and the dice. I handle my dice like I handle my bitches, I keep them on my dick and constantly making dough for me, you dig. As the dice left his hand, he made a swishing sound. The dice glided gracefully toward the floor and ricochet toward me. It was too late to move or to apologize, the damage had been done. The die had struck my feet in slow motion. Lying face up, the dice spit out a one and a two. Duke stepped to me seething with anger. You didn't see me rolling the dice punk, I should punch you in your mouth, he motioned with his fist. His face was contorted in rage. You owe me some money. Swaggering towards me he pointed directly in my face. He stepped nose to nose with me eyeing me down with a menacing glare. He flexed his muscles as he placed his right hand next to my temple. Duke you think I'm playing with you, he raised his left hand, and now had my head sandwiched parallel between both his hands. All eyes in the courtyard were on us and the tension was high. During this whole scenario I stood my ground and didn't flinch. I put my skills through the test and challenged my fears. I stared directly into his eyes piercing his soul. I wanted him to know he wasn't fucking with no punk. Looking directly into my eyes he saw it too, he smiled raising his eyebrow in confused curiosity. This little nigga got heart; he extended his hand to give me a pound. What's your name family. I knew everything that I did from this point would determine

52

whether cats would have respect for me, or whether they would try to play me. My grandfather taught me the rules on how to conduct myself in the company of men. He always told me by shaking a man's hands you can determine the strength of his character, so it was important that you grip his hand and put some power into it, or men will think that you are weak. Who was I to contend with the rules? I listened, learned, remembered and now it was my time to experience. I told him my name and extended my hand and gave him the original Black man soul pound. His hand was swelled up, hard, and calloused. His knuckles were black and ashy. He gripped my hand with power, his nails bit into my hand and were more like claws. I held my composure and passed through the gantlet of thugs showing no emotion. I was tested and prevailed, I had proven myself and would now be considered one of the fellas. He had introduced as kyki. He told me the names of the others, but I really didn't care to know them, I just wanted to keep it moving. Though I lived in the ghetto it was never a part of my lifestyle. Something strange transpired that day, from that day every time I entered the building, I got the head nod from those who dwelled in the lobby. I was now official, and this was my new home.

I quickly adjusted to my new environment, it was the same shit, different day. I remained incognito, minded my business and kept a low profile. I never engaged in gossip, hung in the lobby, smoked weed in the stair well, played dice, drunk forties or chattered about who got shot, who got knocked, and who was fucking who. I always wondered what was the significance of standing all day in front of or inside in a cold lobby in the projects. Perhaps it was a

53

pathological method of male bonding for males who grew up lacking a self-identity. For the ghetto was a dysfunctional matriarchal society controlled by women. Perhaps they were trying to discover the manhood within each of them as they searched for that lost fatherhood which they had never known.

CHAPTER 7 JUNIOR HIGH SCHOOL

Moving back to Brownsville, I began going to Junior High School 263. This school had a reputation that put fear in the hearts of men. It was said that if you were a freshman and were not known you would get fucked up, robbed or have your head dumped in a toilet boil. It was said that students entering this school had to fight every day in order not to get punked. The first day I arrived I peeped all the known stick up kids and thugs that roamed the hallways looking for victims. After graduating from public school my grades were pretty good, I received awards for math and writing and was immersed in an excellent class. My teacher was a stern west Indian educator named Mr. McCoy. He was hated by most because he had a learn or die mentality. He used to tell us as black men and women we had to work two times as hard as everyone to overcome racial discrimination and prejudice. We were young and didn't want to hear most of what he had to say, but I would remember those truths he espoused in my later years. Mr. McCoy saddled us with tons of homework, in addition we had a host of other classes we had to attend. When we complained he used to say you can play your way through life but in this class, you're going to work -there's no two ways about it, and work we did. He taught us how to effectively use mathematics and apply it to our everyday lives, as well as how to read and write with diction and articulate the English language. He told us the way in which we communicate would play an important part of our lives. He told us it would benefit us in the business world which was primarily run by those in the dominant society. He said the way in which we articulated the English language would illustrate what class and economic background we came from. If we could not communicate effectively the world would perceive us as uneducated or lower class. I remember his words to this day because they gave me seeds for thought. I always wondered why those who were most successful spoke the kings English. They even dressed a certain way; they wore business attire and were clean shaven. In America that was the image of success. It was no wonder that the rest of the world thought so little of those who dwelled in the ghetto. In my world that white collar image represented soft, square niggas. If you got caught looking like a chump in my hood you wouldn't make it a block from the train without getting preyed upon. Working people in my neighborhood just went to work and came home and didn't leave their homes, it was real in the battlefield. Marcus had an infamous allure. For students entering their freshman year they were scared shitless. They had heard the rumors and were shitting in their pants on the first day of school. The day most students dreaded was fresh man day. On freshman day most students didn't come to school because they were terrified. Luckily for me I got schooled by my older cousin Black, he was a veteran thug and a predator who used to roam the school hallways testing, robbing, extorting and assaulting students back in the days. He was known in the projects, everyone knew his name and his claim to fame, he was a general in the stick-up game. He took me on the back of a dim the stairwell to run the game down in detail. He stared at me with a lion's gaze as he began to speak. Listen cousin when you step in the yard you always must keep your game face on. When you're in school you got to silence all that laughing and smiling, or they will think you're soft as cotton candy. Black began schooling me regarding the elementary principles of survival like I was sucker on a prison bus on the way to the penitentiary. When you in the yard always keep your back to the fence, be on point, always guard your grill and never sleep. If someone steps to you asking you questions about who you know, tell them you don't know shit. Never let a stranger or potential enemy within arm's reach because they may be planning to strike or assault you. I want you to understand if they start asking you to many questions, they're trying you. They're testing you to see if you're weak or weather you will fold under pressure. If you confess and tell them your name, where you live, who you know, what clothes and shoe size you wear, they will know that you have fear in your heart and you are pussy. They will then extort, rob, beat or clown you in front of your peers. Remember to look them in their eyes, keep your head up, never look down or away that is an indication of fear, stand up for yourself. Let others know you're not one to be fucked with. The sooner you establish your name the sooner you get your fame. If you must fight, then just fight! It doesn't matter whether you win or lose but that you stood like a man; trust me you'll win your respect. I listened mesmerized at the sheer ferociousness of his diction. I knew his words rang true because I felt their power. The irony of it all was these unwritten laws could be applied to the streets as well as the classroom. Black explained that schools were like jails; they had the yard; the mess hall, detention, and security staff to enforce their rules on the student population. But regardless of the appearance of control, weapons were smuggled into the buildings, gangs assembled in their various clicks, and there were incidences of violence on a continual basis. The lessons Black imparted were worth their weight in gold and would prove significantly important to my survival as a young man coming of age in middle school or what I called the lion's den.

CHAPTER 8 FRESHMAN DAY

With freshman day a week away, I felt a sense of anxiety though I was confident that I could handle myself properly. While at home, I committed at least twenty-five minutes a day to shadow boxing in order to hone my skills to a sweet science. I was prepared for anything that might befall me that day. Though I had size, my skills had to be up to par because the big man was always the first cat to be tested. With the day fast approaching, I continued to test my skills. In the hand game it was not who hit harder, but who hit first, and who got hit. In the hand game the main objective is to win, no matter how you must do it. If you had to fight dirty, then you had to do what you had to do. In the hand game no one can tell you to fight by a set of rules as there are none. Fighting was about guts and glory, if you couldn't stand in the arena then don't step into a man's game. As a young man you had to learn how to fight but once you learned it had to become a part of you. I thoroughly prepared myself for freshman day as it was only a matter of time before I would be tested.

It was a beautiful springtime day. The sunshine cast its glorious rays amidst the luscious outgrowth of trees that bloomed surrounding peaked towers which held the poor wretched and forgotten sons and daughters of the Brownsville. Today held promise as well as foreboding. It was freshman day and my emergence into the world of manhood was near. No longer would I be characterized as fresh. Today my mettle would be tested and again I would have to stand.

I awoke showered and dressed. I put on something raggedy because I knew today might be the day. I tied my shoelaces tightly. Taking a deep breath, I exploded throwing five to six jabs at midair. For some reason I was getting butterflies in my stomach. Denouncing my fear, I flexed, tightened, and tensed every muscle in my body pushing out the anxiety which threatened to immobilize me. I left my bookbag on the table. Looking back once more I made sure the house was in order before I ventured out into the cold and ruthless world. I knew today was going to be one of those days, I could feel it in the air. As I strolled towards school, I knew I was going to face some type of shit this morning. I walked along Sutter Avenue. Dope fiends seemed to come out of their nods to eye me in an unnervingly peculiar manner. It was sort of eerie. Groups of teens hung out in the doorway gave me the nod. Was there something I couldn't perceive or was oblivious of? Or was I a lamb walking to the slaughter and everyone were saying their last goodbyes. I met with other freshmen heading toward school and understood what others had seen as I peered in the face of my comrades, I saw unbridled unmasked terror. They walked as if they were on their way to the gas chamber. I guess these were the kids whose mothers demanded that they attend school, others had let their kids remain home fearing their safety. I saw fear in their eyes, had I exhibited the same fear? I approached one of the freshmen. I spoke candidly trying to sound as relaxed an unafraid as possible. I saw through his false façade like a child looking through trace paper. He was trying to act hard in order to mask his insecurities, but he was clearly soft. Now if I was able to clearly see he was pussy trying to act hard, and I'm not a thug or a predator, then imaging what a seasoned predator would see. Clearly, he was in danger of being victimized this afternoon during lunchbreak or afterschool, cause eventually you had to go home and there was only one entrance that students could exit from, that was the southern gate entrance on the Blake avenue side, and believe me thugs had already formulated plans a week in advance as to how they were going to execute mad stick ups on that day. I had to think, I had to come up with a plan just in case shit hit the fan. Thinking one dimensionally, I never contemplated that maybe I might have to fight more than one assailant. I never contemplated the probability that they might have weapons; I never even contemplated bringing weapons of my own in order to ensure my own safety. Cursing myself I started to become hesitant as to whether I should go or to school or do a 360 and return to the safety of my abode. Full of determination I conjured up the strength to carry on. I was only a block away, and besides if I was seen by anyone walking back towards my home, word on the street would be that I myself punked out and was a coward. That couldn't happen because I wouldn't let it go that far, if I was to fight this morning, this afternoon, or this evening I would whip ass like a man or take an ass whipping in a likewise fashion. But regardless what the case would be, brothers would have to respect me in general because I had heart and was willing to go for mines. As I neared the school, I put on my game face just as my cousin black had instructed. I switched into thug mode; I started walking mad hard swaggering like I was the head nigger in charge. I joined the herd of fresh new faces

61

entering the building. These students I guess they were just generally stupid, naïve, or just didn't have any common sense, or maybe it was just me who was just paranoid. But most of the students came dressed to impress and were absolutely fly.

The guys wore fresh lee denim jeans, name plated chains, and belts, suede and leather fronts, Kangal hats and puma sneakers, the girls wore tight fitting spandex jeans, rocked fresh Jerri curls, door knocker earrings, name plated rings on their fingers, and tight-fitting lee jackets in all flavors and colors. I was in awe, and then my awe became embarrassment. Peering at my reflection from the window of a car, I was not amused at what I saw. I was looking shabby as hell, my hair was 'wolf', my clothes were wrinkled, I just had on anything, and I wasn't feeling it. I had to get my shit together. Was I mis-lead, were all the rumors just that, rumors? My peers they seemed to know something that escaped my attention, that first impression count. I guess everybody came to school that day for different reasons. The girls came to school looking sweet as candy in order to impress the popular junior and seniors, they wanted to turn heads and have jaws dropping. The guys came fly to represent; they wanted the fly girls, juniors as well as seniors to take notice. They wanted to show off their dud's in order to let girls know what they were working with. Everybody wanted to see and be seen. Freshman day it seemed as though it was one giant fashion show. Freshman day meant literally what it implied, "fresh-men and women. Students that day were dressed to impress both men and women, to me, it was more of a fashion show, a showcase of fresh meat. They caught the eyes of the student population for sure. But all my preparation and precaution had not gone in vain. For just as the freshmen passed through the gauntlet of Marcus's student body at the gates of the school yard, I saw a posse of Marcus's local thug population. These were the cats who came on school grounds but never attended class. Instead they menaced students in the hallways, robbed them on the stairs, and caused disruptions in other classrooms by barging into classrooms uninvited in order to see their homeboys or their girlfriends. They were serial predators; these cats could smell the fear in a man, and they were notorious for 'sizing up' their victims. My cousin black had schooled me well. I was able to peep thugs in formation before they attacked. They used a strategy that was well deployed against their intended victims.

First, they deployed scouts to check the area for their intended mark. The scout would eye you down ferociously and if you flinched or looked away that was a sign of fear which gave them the green light to set your ass up for the kill. The scout would then step to you and ask you the set off question, like weather you knew some kid. They would name cats in the community everyone knew, and if you stated you knew the dude the scout would go back to his team, and all of them would approach you then the main leader would step to you and tell you some bullshit about how he had beef with the kid for some reason or other and then accuse you of knowing the kid. Then they would tell you because you knew the kid, they were going to make an example of you. They would then stick you up for your money your jewelry, your clothes, and then get in your face and dare you to say something. If you said one word, they would pounce on you and start ragging, snuffing, and raining punches and kicks on you. After they pounded you out, they would then stomp you out. If you were fortunate enough to get up and run, they would spread out in loose formation and just swing on you at will bombarding you with a volley punches in order to rock you knocking you on your ass. I had seen similar incidents like this transpire before. This was the horror I had to live with daily, but this time I was better prepared and aware of the situation, and the environment, so I would not get caught sleeping. Everyone entered the building on time and without incident and all was well that morning, but best believe me mad victims had already been marked and were bound to get stuck during lunchtime or at 3:00 o'clock. Throughout the course of the day an uneasy quiet had settled throughout the school. There was a sense of tension amongst students in the freshman population. I think they were intuitively aware that something was going to happen, but they knew neither the time nor moment in which it was going to transpire.

This was unsettling for some; they looked out the windows, watched their backs, and looked over their shoulders as they left and entered classrooms during different class periods. It was 11:45 and nearing lunchtime. The relative ease of the morning had diminished, and a blanket of tension and fear had covered the classrooms of Marcus freshman student body. It was as if the classrooms had been transformed into holding pens for sheep who were being fattened up to be led to the slaughter; some would escape but not all, many would be sheared, skinned and eaten alive by the wolves-the thugs and predators of Marcus gravy junior high school. It was 12:00 o'clock. The moment of reckoning had arrived. The students nearly shitted on themselves at the sound of the school bell, yet they were very hesitant to move from their seats. Each was waiting for the other to make the first move for the door for logic dictated that it would be he who would be the first to be victimized. And while the intended victim would be getting his ass wiped and robbed this would provide a distraction that would make it easier for the others to escape to the lunchrooms and street below. The school bell began to chime, my heart began beating like a drum. I left Mr. Mc Coys classroom moving silently through the hallways with stealth like a panther. Although I was quite tall for my age, I was able to blend with the crowd remaining virtually unnoticeable. Moving swiftly toward the staircase I passed a throng of juniors who had captured on unfortunate freshman in the hall wall and where leading him to the bathroom, everyone acted as if they had seen nothing. What was strange though was that this freshman although he had been captured, he could have screamed for help, but he chose not to. I would later come to understand that rules of the street applied to the classroom as well. One could not reveal the identity of another who did an injustice towards him or he or she would be forever labeled as snitch. It was a strange rule that I would never understand, because if someone was whipping my ass, I'm telling.

CHAPTER 9 SLAP BOXING

Little did I know that although I donned no jewelry or fly gear worth taking it would be I who would be tested this day. I moved swiftly down the dimly lit stairwell in the end of the school's corridor. Nearing the exit, I rushed through the door into the light of the mid-afternoon sun. It felt good; its rays danced on the surface of my skin. The air wasn't all that necessarily fresh, it smelt like bus fumes from the b-60, but it was ghetto and it was home. Just as I was approaching the gateway, I felt someone behind me. My body tensed, I swung around to meet the impending threat. Our eyes met. His frame six feet five inches, black as hell, full of muscle, smelling of weed and liquor, face of pure stone greeted my glance. Every muscle in my body tensed seeming to freeze in place. Time seemed to stand still for what seemed like an eternity until the silence was broken by his voice which sounded like the roar of thunder billowing from heaven. What's up cuz, your new here, what's your name? His voice was so hard its vibrations alone seemed to make the floor tremble. Cuz, my man over here said he thinks you're a sucker. I looked over my shoulder and saw this tall wiry hard rock with cornrows in his hair shadow boxing, he looked my way. My time had come, once again I had to take my stand as a man. I would have to show an prove once again that my shit wasn't sweet. Within seconds before I could even respond a crowd had gathered, a circle had formed, and I found myself locked in the middle. Raise up bitch! He smiled at me a mouth full of gold blinded me momentarily.

I was a defensive fighter only I was never taught to be an offensive aggressive fighter. Regardless whether open or close the result would be the same someone would win, and someone would lose. Like the blood thirsty mob in the roman coliseums of yesteryear throngs of school kids gathered for the festivities. He began to circle me sizing me up in order to begin his attack. I placed my left foot on the outside of his right one in anticipation for his forward lunge so I could successfully dip and pivot my body to the left and dodge his blow. Raising his hand, he placed them parallel to his face and started moving them in a windshield wiper formation smacking his left elbow with the right palm of his hand, the right elbow with the left palm of this hand. His body swayed in an arc motion from left to right like that ride the pirate ship in Coney Island as he simultaneously went low and smacked the ground. This was the uptown, I had never seen it performed in the streets, it was said that this style was developed in upstate prisons. I had heard the rumors how cats were getting knocked out by those who were skilled in this technique. After smacking the floor, he flew at me at lighting speed and caught me with an open-handed uppercut smacking my chin upwards with his left hand. Truly I was caught off guard as this style was completed unorthodox. He smacked me so hard my teeth rattled, and I almost bit the shit out of my tongue as my head flew back. My lip was bleeding, I had to come up with a method to counteract his offense. Anger replaced the impending fear I had initially felt. I had to control myself and think clearly. This kid had skills and the only way I would gain the upper hand was to calm my mind and think. I reflected on the various defensive maneuvers me and DJ mastered. I would have to use them as well as add a few surprises in order to counteract his unorthodox style. His defenses were down he smirked from overconfidence he thought he had me perplexed. I would play into his game and act like I was stumped by his hand skills and when he got close, I would have a few surprises of my own. He returned to his original stance and started to come at me again.

He slapped his elbows, slapped his knees, went low and slapped the floor. This time he just stayed there and started playing a tune on the sidewalk; this nigga was trying to become famous! He then jumped to his feet threw both his hands in the air and rushed at me. Most niggas would have looked up in order to watch his hands, but I was beginning to catch on to his tactics. I watched his shoulders, and his eyes. Once his shoulders moved, I would evade and counter. Hopefully this strategy would work extremely well in order to effectively throw him off his game plan. He swung his hands down full force in order to slap the shit out the top of my dome piece. Surprising myself I dipped and blocked both incoming blows almost effortlessly; it surprised him too, and instead of coming at me with some fancy shit he just started swinging wildly trying to slap the spit out of my mouth, I now had him. Now angry, he lost his cool and started swinging like a white man. He threw; right hook, left hook, jab, jab, swing. I dipped, dipped, swiped, swiped. Countering with a back hand, I then pimp smacked the shit out of him. There was a great silence in the yard, at that moment the world seemed to stop. All at once the crowd roared, in that moment he was jarred to his senses, now shit was about to get real cause he couldn't just let me get away with smacking fire out of his ass, it would damage his reputation. I stood my ground and was not going to give and inch more without fighting tooth and nail to maintain and hold my fort. He was embarrassed, I felt for him, but I was not about to let him whip my ass in front of everyone and make a fool of me. Today wasn't about pride; it was more about survival of the fittest. As he moved towards me swaying side to side his hands were no longer open, his hands were balled tightly into a fist. I saw it in his eyes, this shit done got real! All that fancy uptown bullshit he was doing before went out the window. It would be easier to defeat him now more than ever because he was angry, and because of his anger he would no longer be able to think clearly.

Although he was bigger and stronger, I would not let him overpower me. He ran at me like a deranged caged animal. I knew he would swing on me with all his might. This would give me a tactical advantage over him because he would throw all his weight with that punch which would leave him open for my counter punch. He responded exactly as I expected. Screaming he swung wildly at me like a white man in a bar brawl trying to hit me with a right. I dipped the punch easily and threw a hard-left jab to his solar plexus. He grunted losing all his wind and breath in his lungs. As he knelt over to catch his breath, I hit him with an elbow to his chin. His head was violently jarred back, at that instant he bit deeply into his tongue. Feeling no pity, I was about to finish him by raining a series of combinations on his head back and neck till he crumbled to the pavement like a deck of cards. Suddenly I felt a hard blow to the back of my head. Falling forward I was assaulted by a series of blows to by head to my back and my face. I curled into the fetal position in order to protect my head and body from this continued onslaught by this group of assailants. They continued to kick, punch and stomp me. He too joined in the rampage stomping on my head as I held it tightly between my two hands in a meager effort to shield myself from these punishing blows. For what seemed like hours they continued to jump me. I had to get my bearings and look for an opening in order to make my break. Finding a weak point in the mass I summoned the last bit of energy I had to make my escape. At that moment I jumped to my feet and swung widely at one of their weak flunkies. As he winched back flinching in terror, I saw a small opening between he and another man. At that moment I rushed forward with all my might viciously breaking through the two. I ran through a gauntlet of 20 to 25 men who in their attempt to capture me ripped the shirt off my back. I ran all the way home non-stop feeling a sense of victory as well as defeat for although I had won the battle that day, I had lost the war. I learned a very important lesson that day; in war one must gain and maintain allies in order to win victories decisively.

Though it had seemed that I took a brutal beating from a crew of thugs, I had made a name for myself in school. From that day forward I didn't have any problems.

In my case I had to experience pain and blood to get what I yearned for the most respect. I got through junior high school without a hitch. I was in my last few months of school. Graduation was approaching and my mind wandered as it always does. I began to ponder the complexities that I would encounter as I entered high school. According to the zoning laws of my district I was slated to attend Wind Gate high school, but I refused for I had heard many harrowing tales of murder, mayhem and brutality. The year was 1983 West Indians were entering New York in mass. The start of a new rising drug culture was emerging, and African Americans would compete for drug territories in east New York, Brownsville, and the other boroughs. The crack epidemic had exploded on the scene with the force of a nuclear bomb. Stick up kids, hard rocks, thugs, players, and underground entrepreneurs, took to the drug trade like flies to warm shit, and it was on. The ghettos of New York became the Beirut's, and Vietnams of the inner city. A war was raging, the combatants were American Blacks, West Indians and Puerto Ricans. The product was crack. Neighborhoods were divided into localities, one crew couldn't sell past Sutter avenue, another past East New York Avenue. In a neighborhood composed of over ten different projects each project had its crew and sold to its customers. Drug wars started when one crew intruded upon the territory of their rivals. Everybody was armed to the teeth. A lot of money was being made. Drug dealers sported Bally's, kangols, rope chains and trunk jewelry on their fingers. They rode Volvos, Mercedes Benzes, Saabs, and luxury cars of all kinds. During the eighties on a yearly basis hundreds of people died in the ghettos per year. Every night gun fire erupted in front of the projects or off in the distance. Every week you would hear tales of who got shot and who got knocked. A cycle of despair had been created that would have a lasting impact on the black community for years to come.

This would be the environment that I would come of age in reaching my maturity. During this pivotal period in my life my self-esteem would be tested, and I would suffer severe trials in my quest for manhood that would forever leave an impression on my psyche.

CHAPTER 10   HIGH SCHOOL BLUES

I graduated from Marcus with honors that year. In September I was slated to attend East New York Vocational High School. I was able to skirt getting zoned into Wingate due to my mother's ability to find loopholes in the system, she was good at that. September was right around the corner and I was about to face a new set of challenges in a new environment amongst a new set of people. My mother felt that this school would be most suited to my best interest since it was an all-boys school that was on the borderline of Brooklyn and queens. She had hoped that I would not encounter the same problems that had previously occurred, this school would provide that chance for me to start anew and meet a new class of people outside of the confines of my ghetto environment. Yes, things would be quite different much different contrary to what she and I both believed it would be. My high school was in East New York the South Central of Brooklyn. It was quietly nestled in the boondocks on the borderline of the Atlantic avenue and north conduit expressway. Unbeknownst to me this school was sandwiched between the notoriously infamous Cypress Hills housing projects which at the time was run by the A-team Brooklyn's most feared drug crew, and Franklin kay Lane high school, a rival school that was embroiled in a continuous war of rivalry which produced casualties on the Brooklyn as well as the Queens side of the fence. Either way you could catch a beatdown arriving to school or departing school. Most of the people who were assaulted took the J train and got caught on the predominantly Puerto Rican side of town. Other victims got caught riding the back of the A train during the school rush hour and got stomped out by wolf packs, groups of teens who marauded in groups of 20 and 30 who preyed on students for fun or to acquire gains such as money or jewelry.

So, I was caught up in a new set of circumstances because in East New York High School you had sets and clicks who had allegiance both to cypress and to the Puerto Rican liberty avenue crews in the area. In a sense Marcus was just a training ground for the real thing. Symbolically I had left boot camp and was now in Vietnam and had to move like a soldier to escape the killing fields of the projects. It was 1985, yet the only people fortunate to live large were the players, ballers, and hustlers. Virtually everyone wanted to be a drug dealer and make fast money. It was a quick way to get rich and have the money, the girls, the clothes, and the gold. It was black America's equivalent of the American dream. Gone were the days when black men pulled themselves up by their bootstraps worked two jobs and saved their pennies in order to get a house in their mid-forties. It was the 8o's these were the Reagan years; blacks were caught dead broke and empty handed and found themselves in the middle of a nationwide recession. There were hardly any jobs making what would be considered a respectable living. The only jobs that were in abundance were those which required little if no mental effort, jobs that a monkey could be trained to do, like messenger work, security, or a professional burger flipper, you might as well be slave labor because the most they were paying was $1.25 per hour, with this type of pay you would be lucky if you could get Chinese food and a pack of toilet tissue let alone pay bills. So the rush began, Blacks from the age of 15-35 years of age dropped from the school system in mass numbers the job market also showed a decrease in African American employment and the working class and poor masses of black humanity flocked to the green oasis's in the inner city ghettos in search of that white gold that made the fortunes and dreams of men come true, they were in search of crack dreams.

To say the least the recession influenced black spending power that year and I was feeling it. I was fucked up, my shoes were talking the soles were run down on both sides like ice skates, I had an old brown pleather jacket that was peeling at the elbows and faded out tight ass pin stripe lee's, and I sported a kinky uneven afro. Yet I was expected to make due with what I had because times were hard. Moms knew I was in need and she tried to make due she bought me a pair of red Puma's a couple of pair of pants and some school supplies. She brought me some shirts too, but they were all short sleeves because she was unable to afford long sleeve shirts which were the same price as adult men's shirts. I had also grown considerably during the summer months after going upstate to the fresh air fund taking in that fresh air and eating that bland ass food. I was now 6'2' and I was changing, my voice got deeper I got hair on my dick; shocked the hell out of me, but I did. But I was still growing into my body and it would take some time before I felt comfortable. I was suffering from self-esteem issues that I had to resolve. I watched other boys become men; they did so by engaging in social activities and sports like basketball, football, weightlifting boxing and rapping to girls. But is had a dilemma is didn't engage in sports of any kind and is was quite shy. Sports in effect during a man's adolescent years provided a means male bonding and friendship. Where would that leave me, friendless, or an outcast? These were the questions that is contemplated as is prepared to make my transition into high school. I was basically a bundle of contradictions. I didn't know whether I was coming or going. I felt on the one hand I was grown; on the other hand, I was still a child. I would try to solve my dilemma on my own, yet I needed someone to talk to. I didn't want to confide in my mother for I wanted to stand as a man on my own two feet. I guess this testosterone flowing through my veins swelled my head as well as my balls cause I wanted to do it all alone although I didn't have a pot to piss in or a window to throw it out of, dig!

This would be the first time I would be stepping on my school campus. Officially it was the first day of high school, of course I nervous as hell I had butterfly's in my stomach and my hands were clammy and moist. This was a whole new experience for me I boarded the A train at Broadway Junction going towards far rockaway that was a first. I had never taken that route before. To me it seemed awkward as if I were moving backward in time and space. It was a completely different crowd that frequented the train on this route. Always very observant, I noticed the amount of black people decreased as we moved closer to my destination. Damn what had my mother gotten me into, I pondered. Was I going to be in an all-Spanish environment? Fuck it, I couldn't worry about the small things I had much bigger fish to fry, it was the first day of school and I had to access my new accommodations and find a way to fit in although my life was a piece that could only fit into my puzzle. The train roared furiously down the tunnel toward Euclid Avenue I had a habit of always riding in the front of the train. I loved to look out the window into the tunnel it was an exciting and invigorating way to beat the monotony of subway travel. As the train approached Euclid avenue station, I took my toothbrush wiped the soil off my puma sneakers, tied my laces, pated my small afro and stood up. The train came to a grinding halt. I threw my bookbag across the small of my back as I high stepped along the platform. As I neared the stairwell the light of the morning sunshine greeted my glance. It was warm an inviting for a moment I forgot all my fears and anxieties and I was caught up in the beauty of the moment. Like have you ever walked and daydreamed simultaneously and be so enthralled in your fantasy that you didn't realized that you had stopped breathing and you were holding your breath, it was sort of like that.

As I walked along Pitkin Avenue the ghetto held me in its iron embrace. Looking around I concluded at that moment that all ghettos were essentially the same in composition they were dirty rundown and the people were poor, and always at its foundation lied people of color, mostly black and brown. There were a throng of students headed towards the school I followed them at a reasonable distance to find my way as I traveled towards my destination. My anxiety began to subside after I began to see other people, I recognized from my neighborhood heading towards my new school. As I neared the school grounds it looked more like the academies I had seen on television. The school was two blocks long its radius about four blocks

77

wide. East New York Vocational High School it had its own airplane hangar and automobile garage. The school also had its own hand ball and basketball courts. And its own football and baseball fields. To say the least I was very impressed. This new school greatly surpassed all my expectations, it boasted of its exclusive number of programs in electronics, computers, automotive and carpentry. The student body was made up of a diverse population of Asian whites and Middle Eastern peoples, but blacks and Latinos were the majority. The blacks were from all over Brooklyn; many were from East New York and Brownsville others were from Bedford Stuyvesant. The Hispanics were mostly from Bushwick and East New York. By general observation I ascertained the dynamics of the student body politic. You still had clicks that hung out on the school grounds and in the auditorium before the start of the morning classes. The brothers hung out with cats from the neighborhood sometimes you had a couple of cool Puerto Ricans who hung with the brothers and brothers who hung with Puerto Ricans. The nerds, the foreigners and the outcast generally hung together in clicks too. Coincidentally I was grouped amongst this category because I wasn't Mr. Popularity, I didn't know the known niggas and I was not known. I didn't play ball and was not a playa. I felt very awkward around fly girls, I sweated stuttered and became clumsy. I was still in my ugly duckling stage, but one day I knew I would become a swan.

The first few weeks of high school I was in a slump, I guess I had problems adjusting to my new environment. It wasn't scared of nothing, I guess was suffering from homesickness. For a while I became a loner , I didn't hang out with anyone, I went to lunch outside of the school for a time until I finally got my book of lunch tickets so I could eat in school because lunch was not free you had to pay for it. Those who could not afford to pay either brought their lunch from home or starved all day till they got home, I was one of those unfortunate ones who fell into that category. Those who were fortunate enough to receive lunch stipends often got robbed swindled or coned for them by thugs, hustlers, or card sharks in dice games or other frivolous endeavors. In a way the lunch book became a form of currency in my school. Cats traded cigarettes and other goods for lunch tickets. I made sure I only brought one ticket per day because if I lost my book, I would have to wait for three months or more in order to receive a new one, and that was a gamble my stomach couldn't afford to take. In time I met new friends although they weren't the most popular or most known cats in school, I had somebody to vibe with during school hours. One of the coolest cats I would meet out of my medley of associates was this cat named Jose. Jose was from Tilden projects, he lived on the Mother Gaston side of the tenements. He was a laid-back cat, but I guess he wasn't wild enough to roll with the thugs, so he hung with me and a few other dudes. I never wanted to be classified or labeled or placed in a box, I just wanted to be me. I knew I was somebody, after linking up with Jose he introduced me to the rest of his click in East New York high school.

I was introduced to my new family during lunch period. That was the time most enjoyed by students during the day. If a student failed mostly everything in his school the easiest class to pass was gym and lunch. In my view the lunchroom was a microcosm of society. It wasn't a melting pot where all groups freely intermingled with each other during grub time, the lunchroom was clearly demarcated. It was separated into different zones and spheres of influence. You had the Puerto Ricans, the Mexicans and all the groups who shared the Spanish language occupying the western perimeter. The Blacks from various neighborhood such as East New York, Brownsville and Bedford Stuyvesant occupied the central perimeter of the lunchroom. Finally, you had the outcast they were what you would call the melting pot. There were individuals who derived from the other two groups. The outcast was composed of Blacks, Puerto Ricans, Mexicans, Indians, a hand full of white boys and a smattering of Asians. We all shared one thing in common we didn't fit with the in crowd. The popular, the known, the respected and the feared were amongst this group, these were the players the thugs the hustlers the ballers and shot callers. In our case we were those who didn't fit into any of those categories. In a way we were freer than all the other more popular groups, we didn't have to go through the stress of living up to others expectations, we didn't have to keep up with the fads and styles and we didn't have to conform to the peer pressure being exerted by members in our social circles. We were all free-thinking individuals who were leaders unto ourselves. There was no leader in our group everyone did his or her own thing, and it was respected. We were into comic books, drawing, video games, actions figure and science fiction. The gist of our conversation at lunch time consisted of this subject matter.

After I was formerly introduced, I began to hangout forming loosely associated relationship with my new friends. My high school experience was now much less lonely due to my new social affiliations. In almost every class I attended I saw at least two of my friends. My first year in high school I attended various shop and carpentry classes, computer courses, and foreign language classes. I got into the daily routine of school life, but I was bored and depressed, my grades during the first marking period sadly reflected this fact. Although I claimed I didn't give a fuck what others thought about me, I was sadly deluding myself. Subconsciously my physiological protective mechanism was wearing thin. I could bullshit everyone else in the whole world but when I looked in the mirror at night, I couldn't bullshit myself. I wasn't no outcast, I wasn't a nerd, I was just misunderstood. I wanted popularity, I wanted people to know my name, I wanted chicks, mommies, honey's, but I didn't have the money or resources. I had to deal with the hand I was dealt, and I had to start from the bottom. I couldn't deal with the fact that I had no status, I was damn near invisible I walked amongst others literally unseen and literally unfelt-that shit fucked me up. I was in deep contemplation pondering a means to extract myself from this situation. Every lunch time I would assess these cats I found myself associated with, they had absolutely no game or social skills, I wasn't the most street-smart cat myself but at least I had potential.

On different occasions I used various methods of game that had been taught to me to my advantage. On the other hand, these cats were lame as shit. I observed them on many occasions and wondered to myself the various reasons why cats did every and anything in their power to achieve status-even die to achieve it-it was for this reason. I looked at this medley of misfits in their social interactions and shook my head and wondered do I look like this when seen by others.

I peeped my so-called crew, mother fuckers had members only jackets on with dockers pants, no haircut and glasses with fucking tape on it. Shit I wasn't that fucked up. I was going through my adolescent transition into manhood. I was growing into myself, but since I yet didn't know and understand who I was I suffered from a low self-esteem. They say that a person's friends reflect who he or she is. Aggressive types hang with thugs, outgoing types hang with the popular crowd, and those who are shy, reserved and unpopular hang with nerds or outcast. I didn't fit any one's mold or classification; I was a mixture of all these things at one time or the other. Although I didn't agree with the category, I was placed in for the mean time I was in no position to change my circumstances because I didn't have the necessary tools of the trade in which to ply my craft, mainly the car, fly clothes, and the jewelry, that would come much later. I would play the role for now, but I would always be cognizant of any opportunity which arose that would give me the chance to better my position in life. I would chill on the humble and play the silent role remaining ever watchful keeping abreast of the current trends and the word on the street, for those who remained on the bottom could only rise to the top and those on top could only fall. While I was at the bottom, I would learn the lessons conducive to keeping me on the top, never taking for granted my position, never forgetting where I came from. It was these mistakes that made the players get played, the ballers lose the ball and the thugs become victims. I knew that one day my time would come, and I would be ready to shine like the light of the sun during the noon day.

CHAPTER 11   THE LUNCHROOM

Besides the sorrows and the pains of adjusting to high school life during the height of my adolescence there were many joys and memories of high school which leave its impression indelibly etched forever in my mind. One on those such memories that come to the fore is the lunchroom, it was here that dreams were made, and the lives and reputations of men were laid. In the lunchroom cats came in their Sundays best freshly dressed, denims pressed, fresh sneakers, chains freshly shined with their heads faded, flat-topped, Caesar, and well groomed. This is where they showcased their gear. This was the ghetto cabaret where smooth players gamed honey toned chicks wearing those tight dresses that hugged their hips. This arena was for fly and those who were live. If your game was not tight your best bet was to play the corner and keep your mouth shut, cause I have seen many a man played out dissed and dismissed by fly chicks and down ass bitches; and let a nigga raise up trying to flip, that would be his ass, cause bet your bottom dollar she knew all the hard rocks thugs and crews in the school, by 3:00 o'clock your ass would either be beat the fuck down or cut the fuck up; your choice. Lunch for me began from 1:00 o'clock to 2:00 after going through the daily routine medley of classes during the morning I quietly eyed the clock waiting in anticipation for the school buzzer to sound off signaling grub time. My stomach was burning like

I drank a vat of acid I didn't have time to eat breakfast because I woke up late, and if I missed lunch, I would have to boil potatoes or make poverty pancakes-that shit you made with flower and water when you had nothing else to eat at home. The end of the period had arrived. I burst from my seat like I was running track and field at the Olympic semifinals. I didn't give a fuck what anyone thought although quietly I witnessed the stares and the snickers of those who thought I must have been a starving ass nigga...I was!

I silently flowed with the current of rowdy students who nosily moved through the hallways like a throng of cattle their chatter resounding in bellows symbolically like the mowing of cows rushing to the feeding trough. I ran into my man Jose who I hadn't seen in a while, actually I was playing low profile until I got my shit together, and quiet as kept I tried to keep my distance away from the crew of misfits who quietly embraced me since my arrival to this new school. Jose! I grasped his hand with power and gave him a soul pound at least he had that down pack.

What's up big bro, he patted me on the shoulder, and punched me playfully in my chest. I'm chilling, I tried my best not to meet his gaze for fear of him noticing my unease. Ale you alright man I haven't seen in since god knows when man, cats thought you got locked up or something. I shrugged my shoulders, I just been chilling, keeping it moving, I shifted uneasily placing both my hands in my pocket. The crew has been asking about you, they would be mad surprised to see you kid, Jose exclaimed. You going down to the cafeteria, right? It was too late Jose had asked the question gave me the invite and I couldn't refuse his gesture. From that point me and Jose proceeded downstairs in silence. I listened to Jose update me on the gossip, the fights and daily bullshit. I really didn't care too much to hear about. After a while I just toned him out because I'm just not used to hearing men cackling like bitches. Finally, we arrived at the end of the stairwell where everyone was assembled in order. Here we had to wait to be sent in two at a time; like we were in a club or something. I still remember the shit my cousin told me about school and its likeness to prison, the similarities were striking. The thugs the popular cats and the players could skip the line and get in first. They had VIP status because they gave cigarettes and did small favors for the monitors. Sometimes the monitors used to hit these niggas off with whole books of lunch tickets, don't ask me where they got it from, but they got it, and they used to barter and trade books for cash cigarettes or sometimes even a bag of weed on the down low.

We were ushered through the doors into the lunchroom by the monitors finally we were in the arena. The roar of the crowd nearly brought you to your knees as you entered the crowded busy cafeteria enclosure. I always felt self-conscious as I walked by throngs of tables with fly mommy's busy chatting away talking about everything and everybody. These chicks didn't care, if you weren't up to par, they were going to let you know, they were blunt. Or they would look at you from head to toe as you passed, and bust out into hysterical laughter, it was humiliating. My self-esteem was already on the rocks I didn't need no women to crush my pride any further. I moved quickly to my table. I gave everybody a pound, took off my backpack and placed it under the table. I didn't have to worry too much about anybody stealing my bag was it was damn near ripped to shreds from months of wear tear and constant usage. I had gotten used to eating by myself after weeks of lying low, but it felt kind of good being with my comrades. I know they were kind of bugged out, but it was home. Jose pointed out this light skin cutie about 5"4' mad thick… her legs were polished and shining like a freshly cut oak table legs. Her ass began at the small of her back. I never spoke to shorty in my life, but I had seen her in a couple of my classes. I was in love. I never said one word to this chick, and I was strung out already. It was funny how my man pointed her out to me, had he known how I felt? Was it that apparent? I guess it was mere coincidence. She had a slight round face cute luscious lips deep penetrating almond colored eyes and she looked humble and sweet as though she had not been corrupted by the world. She sat with the popular click by virtue of her beauty. She wasn't wild and she didn't talk vulgar or loudly, she was just laid back and cool. She smiled a lot; her smile was beautiful she could make flowers grow from the sunshine and warmth emitted from her sensuality.

I wasn't the only one who felt this way, thugs used to try hard to push up on her, they promised her the world, they promised to take care her, all to no avail because, she just wasn't into materialistic bullshit. I had told Jose that I was feeling shorty, but I was to shook up and shy to pursue my ambitions to be her man. Besides she had turned down the popular players and fly niggas, I fathomed I wouldn't have a chance with her. My man the only way you're going to find out whether you got a chance or not is if you step to her man, said Jose. He was right, but who was he to tell me who I should step to or not, he never had a girlfriend in his life, the closest he ever been to a girl was porno mag. I was shy and my game was not tight at all because I didn't practice rapping to girls on a regular basis, but for this cutie I would be willing to try. I watched, viewed and observed other brothers in action when they rapped to members of the opposite sex. I watched their body language how a brother conveyed his interest in a female was with his eyes. I observed the difference in gazes, one gaze meant could I fuck you now on the stairs or wherever, the other meant could I get to know you better so I could get to fuck you in time. Each gaze was subtle and conveyed its own message, but the funny thing about it was that women were masters at reading them all. They knew who was attracted to them, they knew when you were watching them, they knew if you only wanted to fuck them, and they knew if you were lying or trying to game them, they could spot that shit a mile away. But I had to try; I practiced in the mirror at home what I would say to her. I wrote my lines on paper and memorized them so I could appear to be on top of game. Looking in the mirror my reflection peering directly at me I saw every nook and cranny in my skin it made me self-conscious, but fuck it the only way I would overcome my fear would be to directly confront it; what was my fear you may ask , my fear was what most men feared during their teen years- rejection, I already thought I was fuck up I didn't need a woman; one of those fly beautiful mother fuckers to confirm it, that shit would crush me and make me into a shell of a man. But what was I now if not a shell? I had no choice but to confront and conquer the source of my anxiety- beautiful women.

Returning to school the next day I had my rap properly prepared, I had to get my confidence up I would have until

1:00 o'clock to do so and then afterwards if I succeeded or failed in my undertaking all I could say was that I tried. I got my hair cut into high low fade-a bowl cut if you will, shit what do you expect in 1985, but anyway, my pants were freshly creased I had right guard on, cause a motherfucker had to smell type descent, ma dukes gave me a couple of dollars, so I wouldn't be using the lunch tickets today. Today I would be taking one of the greatest steps in my life since learning to walk, I would be embarking on getting some pussy, and I was as ready. I had told my man my plans, he was all for me he had my back one hundred percent although he had some misgivings about the success of my strategy. I had reasoned that if I write down what to say all would be smooth sailing from there. I never contemplated her responses she could say some shit that my throw my whole plan into turmoil I would have to adlib and adjust the conversation to her response, it just wasn't as cut and dry as I had contemplated. The stress of the whole encounter was beginning to unnerve me, I was having second thoughts, maybe I should just call the whole thing off I reasoned. I couldn't do it because I would be conceding to defeat, and I refused to stay down. I would face shorty like a man and speak my peace, if I got dissed then I got dissed, but least I could give myself credit for trying new bold and courageous things. Throughout the course of the morning classes I daydreamed of the things I would say. I memorized all the lines I had wrote up, and they were pretty good ones at that. Everybody had to start off somewhere, all those players had to learn the game just as I was now doing, all it took was constant repetition and practice, trial and error. Eyeing the clock, I anxiously anticipated engaging in the mating dance that would pit me in a battle of the sexes. The time had arrived, it was 1:00 o'clock the beating of my heart replaced the gong of the school bells. I popped my collar primed and groomed my hair and got up from my chair. My peers eyed me curiously for they had seen in me a sense of new-found bravado for usually I would be quite the recluse sitting in the back of the classroom.

I got up, but each step seemed to me to be a task that required laborious effort on my part. It was if my legs were glued to the floor, but I had to trudge on. I pondered the power of pussy and its enormous potential to heal the world as well as destroy it. I was yet another victim of its powerful vices. I was young and the dam of my suppressive emotions could no longer hold my hormones in check. My sex drive was on overload, and though I was deftly afraid of these new and frightening sensations I was undergoing, I was enthralled and fascinated by the allure of where my dick might lead me. I met up with my man Jose and my other friend David; I used to just call him Dixon. We met on the way to the lunchroom. Eyeing me from head to toe Jose exclaimed, "my man you are looking kind of sharp, you going to church or to court". I ignored his comment, he saw the seriousness of my expression and tersely remarked, shit you must be going to a funeral" no longer able to hide his quivering grimace he and David bust out in uproarious laughter. Alex I'm just messing with you, you look good. Lightening up a bit I blushed at the complement and abruptly blurted out my secret. Bro guess who I'm going out with today. Who, cried Jose? You know that caramel shorty, thick as a brick house and sexy. Oh, shorty you had your eye on for the longest, man you better stop playing cause if you slow you blow. I ignored his statement I had to keep focus and not lose my confidence the time was now, and I was going to step up to the plate like a man and hopefully make it to first base. We stepped into the lunchroom; it was like an arena it seemed as if though there were throngs of spectators on hand to view the festivities. It was as if everyone knew today was my day of recognizing and they were there to either cheer or jeer.

The world seemed to move in slow motion as I my eyes scoured the room in search of her. I scanned every minute detail in the lunchroom, the faces, the gestures, the hand movements, the colors, shapes, and smells in search of her. My heart fluttered and my stomach filled up with so many butterflies I thought I would shit on myself. All at once the world came to a screeching halt. At that moment I neither heard, thought, nor felt anything. The only thing my eyes laid transfixed upon was her. It was as if my senses were heightened, the smell of her smooth soft freshly feminine showered body sent warm chills running up and down my spine; she was bad! But the fucked-up thing was that in that instant I got shook, my mouth and throat got so dry my voice transformed into a whisper and I started perspiring, streams of sweat ran down my arms, legs, and head, damn! I got up from the table and went to the bathroom to get my shit together. Dosing my face with water I stared deeply into the mirror. Closing my eyes, I carefully recited my game lines repetitiously. Looking again at my reflection I spoke aloud and pepped myself. You got this baby it aint nothing, I threw to right jabs at the bathroom wall and banged on my chest in order to feel the pain and gain some sort of modicum of confidence. I stepped out of the bathroom and put on my best hard rock swagger as I bebopped towards the table. Jose looked at me, gesturing with his eyes he pivoted his head in the direction of shorty. "You going step to her or what- huh". I guess he saw through my facade. I had to continue fronting in order to save face. "Nigga I got this, I got this", my mouth was talking but my body was not responding to its message. I had to come up with a method of approach that was both smooth and yet subtle and not to apparent, I had to come off as natural when I spoke with her. My shit couldn't sound coerced or artificial, but as to how I would do it that was the question I had to resolve-how. She got up, my dick throbbed, and my heart was pounding. She moved across the floor with the grace of a panther and with the elegance of a young fawn or gazelle; she had niggas in awe of her. Smooth cats even took notice just to catch a glimpse of the rhythmic and methodical sway of her lovely hips.

As I returned to the table I sat and zoned out for a minute the tumult of the cafeteria faded as I tuned out the roar of the mob. I had to think quickly of a way to approach her without seeming desperate. I pondered several various approaches and narrowed it down to three through the process of elimination. Eureka!!! I got it! Out of the three this approach would be more likely to work than all the others so I would put my best foot forward and give it a try. I figured shorty had some type of cheddar because she never used lunch tickets; she was the type who always brought lunch. I observed her daily routine and I would use it to my advantage to seize the opportunity to get to know her better. Like a lion I carefully observed my prey in silence in leu of the moment I planned to pounce and strike. I was focused and concentrated I saw through the confusion, people, noise

91

and chaos as I watched for an opening. The instant she got up I pounced forward from the table. I was graceful smooth and subtle in my movements. Every muscle in my body pulsed with vitality as I skillfully glided toward my destination. As shorty was in the lunchrooms store buying cholate milk, I moved closer in anticipation for the moment of truth. It was true what they said how milk did a body good cause shorty body was thick and caramel and creamy. I wasn't eating pussy at the time but if I got her she would be first on my list. She didn't notice my approach; she was busy doing what she did best spend money. Everything she did was so feminine. She even took extra care picking her milk as though it really made a difference. I stepped to her I was very careful that my approach wasn't too obvious. She saw me from the side of her eye and clocked me from head to toe in 3.5 seconds; it's a talent that most women have mastered. I walked past her and eyed the deserts acting as though I didn't notice how visibly stunning, she was. I knew I was nervous, but I must have started bugging out or something I started hearing a drum roll. It must have been all in my head, because I knew my time had come, it was now or never. I opened my mouth to speak for a moment, but nothing came out. I'm glad she didn't peep that cause at the time her back was turned.

I mustered up the courage to open my mouth a second time this time I was successful. The words began to flow from the inner depths of my belly echoing through my throat past my esophagus vibrating like harp strings on my vocal cords and at last escaping through my oral cavity. Like an arrow I prayed my words would hit its target. I approached and stated, is there a special type of cholate milk you prefer because I always see you carefully select the perfect carton, I flashed a mouth full of teeth. She gave me a strange inquisitive look, I guess she was trying to figure me out. So far so good I was still here, I lasted longer than most cats who claimed they were players damn I was good.

She began to reply, I watched her young soft and supple lips part gently echoing words sounding like music, they were more beautiful than anything I had heard before. She exclaimed, my mother always taught me to choose quality over quantity, she told me to take my time and choose wisely and I would always make the right decisions in anything I did in life. Damn that was deep, I wouldn't get the full understanding of her statement until later in my life, I now knew why she dissed and dismissed so many who had come across her path she had it all beauty, body, and most of all brains. She had me on my toes I had to definitely think outside the box to fuck with her. I exclaimed, if you like quality over quantity then maybe one day you might consider going to this diner on linden Blvd., I forget the name, but I heard they have the best milk shakes this side of town. She eyed me carefully looking for the routine signs of game being displayed- she found none. I continued, maybe one day you could go there and see for yourself the food is slamming take my word for it. I was masterful in my word play, had I used the word we she would have cut me down with her verbal sword reducing me to half the man I knew I could be. She continued to examine me for any hint of deception, yet she was unable to read me because the difference between me and other cats who tried to "pull" her was they were players and I was not. I smiled and began to run my game I had so carefully practiced for the last few days.

Moving with a natural gait and poise that exhibited no hint of sexual intention or inuendo I exclaimed oh I'm sorry for being so disrespectful I usually don't just talk to just anyone without introducing myself, by the way my name is Alex". I reached out extending my hand to meet hers; this natural acting shit was working like a charm. She extended her hand forward touching mine, I had to keep my composure, or I was sure to nut in my pants; her hand was small and soft like a motherfucker. I continued, are you in Mr. Kowalski's class I thought I saw you there a couple of times. I get him in the afternoons, he has me bugging out sometimes cause he's so old he looks like he about to die or something. Acting silly, I started walking like a mummy and we both bust out laughing. Looking from the corner of my eye I peeped around the room and saw cats checking me out. I had to keep a calm and cool demeanor in order to maintain my confidence cause if I started getting nervous one mistake could fuck up all my plans and I wasn't about to start from ground one again when I had made it so far in such a short length of time. I had her, her psychic defenses were down, she was more relaxed, and she wasn't looking at me with suspicion, that's when I hit her with the master stroke. In order to solidify in her mind, the notion that I truly wasn't trying to push up I turned around as if I was about to walk away without asking her name, I was playing stupid. I turned around I approached her, and I now had an inquisitive look on my face I came back and exclaimed, I'm sorry I didn't get your name. She in turn sarcastically replied, I didn't give it. Then smiling with a devilish grin, she began to laugh. My name is Sherina I'm just messing with you. I was looking in her eyes saying to myself I wish you were messing with me. I quickly peered to the left and saw my niggas at the table excitedly gesturing to me giving me thumbs up for holding it down, I felt like the man. I had surpassed everyone's expectation even my own. So called players were in disbelief for I had gotten more play than the lot of them ever dreamed of.

I had to continue to play it cool and not get caught up in the hype of the moment for all eyes were now on me, and they were looking for me to make a mistake. At this point it would be foolish to suddenly stress her for her phone number in order to impress the knuckle heads who silently watched from afar. I would not set myself up to make the same mistake that all the others had made before me, I would be more patient and use charm and finesse, not game. Had I rushed as other had done she would have automatically been on to me and shut me down. I reached down and pulled a couple of dollars out my pockets. Coyly I mused over the contents of the menu in the cafeteria's store in order to briefly cut our conversation short in order not to appear to anxious. I brought a chocolate éclair and tucked it under my arm in order to put my dough back into my pocket. I casually walked back over to Sherina to conclude our conversation. Sherina it was nice meeting you and remember if you ever want to try out that restaurant, I'll give you the address whenever you're ready, all right, I flashed all my pearly whites. When I'm ready to go you'll be the first person I'll call- see you later, she peered deeply into my eyes and gave me a beautiful smile. We both parted ways walking into opposite directions. As I headed back to the lunchroom table my boys widely gestured with their hand's eyes and heads for me to get shorty's phone number. I paid them no mind, for like the hunter it was best to wait and be patient for your prey to come to you, the kill or capture would be assured. I didn't have mad game like others, but I watched the game for quite some time and I knew how it was played. Women -if they had class-would not want their business in the street, they didn't want to look cheap. From years of observing game I knew if I stepped to her, even if my game was tight, I would not bag her. To many eyes, to many ears, and too many mouths were in the cafeteria. It was a known fact that only easy bitches -the type who got the train ran on them- got bagged in the lunchroom. Choice females would never give up their number or give a nigga play in the lunchroom to many eyes were on them. I had to bide my time and wait for another opportunity to arise- and it wasn't in the lunchroom.

One thing I knew was certain to a woman appearance as well as reputation meant everything to them, it determines whether they were respected or disrespected, if a woman gave the impression that she was a hoe she would be disrespected and treated like one. So, I understood why shorty wouldn't give anybody the play, and it was for that reason that everyone had the highest level of respect for her because her reputation was flawless. Just as a man's word was his bond, a woman's reputation was hers.

As I returned to the table, I didn't even get a chance to sit before Jose and the rest of my crew pounced on me asking me a barrage of stupid questions. Ale did you bag her huh, asked my man Manny. Did you get the number, tell me something man, Jose exclaimed excitedly? I shrugged my shoulders and sighed, no man. All at once the table exploded into an uproar. Aww man you had her and you let her slip through your fingers. Everyone at the table voiced and expressed their disapproval waving their hands and sucking their teeth at my supposed stupidity, but little did they know I had a long-term plan. You mean to tell me you were this close to the pussy and you let it slip through your fingers, man it couldn't be me, exclaimed Manny. Jose saw that I was starting to get visibly agitated so he stepped in interceding on my behalf. He got more balls than all of us, especially you Manny, you might not even have no balls at all. At that moment everyone at the table exploded into uncontrollable laughter, even Manny had to laugh. Jose hugged me and pulled me to the side. Alex for real give me the run down on what really went down, he exclaimed. Sensing the seriousness in his voice I kept it real with him.

Jose, I had to play it cool man I'm not going play my position and pull my own card so shorty could play me out, you know what I mean. I continued, sometimes you got to treat pretty chicks like they aint all that cause everybody else be sweating them and that's what they expect-to be sweated but since my approach was different and original-and I wasn't running lines she might have heard before- I guess she might have been intrigued. So, for a while I'm going to have to play it on the friendship tip till she opens up completely to me then I'm going to make my move". Jose listened and hung on to my words because I was talking some real shit -I guess I was schooling him. "see the reason why most cats don't get love when they approach these chicks is because they be acting hungry, and chicks can spot a dog a mile away. But when you step to them on the humble

97

and just be yourself and don't try to talk some smooth shit or bop hard it doesn't raise a woman's defenses. Yo Ale that's some real live shit you kicking, said Jose. I'm surprised you not a player for real, where did you learn that shit from", he exclaimed. I got a lot of shot callers in my family, who used to be pimps, players, and bosses, and they told me a thing or two about the game, but I never applied what I learned until now. But bro I'm still young to the game and I'm not in a rush, it's about quality not quantity, I ran that line Sherina ran on me to drive home my point and my man Jose must have been feeling what I said cause for the remainder of the lunch period he was lost in deep thought. As fate would have it me and Sherina became cool, I got to know her very well and she and I had a lot in common- too much in common. Her mother was very protective of her and kept her sheltered, she was not a street girl at all, her mother was very stern and strict, she kept Sherina in the books. She wanted to make sure her daughter was well educated so she would not suffer the same fate as her peers- welfare, teenage pregnancy, and adult poverty. Suffice it to say I never got the pussy, but we remained friends. I learned two lessons from the experience: one I had potential to be a young boss or player, two, I could be friends with a woman without seeking to bed her.

I found the high school experience prepared me for various other situations that I was to encounter in my later years. It was there that I went through my transition from childhood to manhood. It was there that I realized that I was at the crossroads in terms of my development as an individual. I was growing older and I had begun to socialize with the opposite sex. I was changing, I began to think differently, I felt it. I had begun pondering my goals and the purpose of my life. I even dealt with situations differently than I might have years ago. Though I was still the average student I was now more well-adjusted to school life; I had my social circle-awkward as they were-I had a few female friends-although I wasn't fucking yet-and I was happy for now. Same shit was still going on, you had the drug dealers, the fights, the he says- she says... you know... the average bullshit, that was expected.

CHAPTER 12   WILDING

The most memorable events recalled in my vivid gallery of thoughts were the subterranean wars fought by black males in search of their identity during the eighties. The wilding era, a time characterized by fear and chaos, was a time in which the law of the streets ruled. This code of ethics dictated that a man's aggressive prowess and will to survive gave him the right to be master and lord in the land of the predator vs. The prey. Under this law, survival of the fittest had precedence over the rule of law and order. Under this code a man hands and his skills at using them classified him as the master of his own environment. Those who remained at the top were those who were dominant in their ability to dish out pain and ferocious violence in unlimited proportions to those they deemed their adversaries. Men of this caliber became thug generals during the wilding era. They also had colonels, sergeants and thug soldiers, it was these soldiers who had to put in work robbing, cutting, busting niggas shit and boot stomping mother fuckers out. This form of chaos was brutally efficient and had a cold cruel order to it. Its purpose served those who wrought this carnage.

The term "wilding" was coined during the eighties and referred to a group of 10 or more youths who ran in "wolf packs" and generally menaced, harassed, robbed, beat, cut, and brutalized anyone of their choosing-for fun that is. These groups of wild men numbering at minimum 10, at maximum 50 or more, were the disaffected dispossessed members of society. They were considered the criminal element; they were society's sociopaths, its undesirable class. They were those considered a menace to 'so called' civilized society. The violence they inflicted on society was the result of its rejection of them. In a twisted irony it was their way of exacting revenge subconsciously by righting the wrongs perpetuated by society in its arrogance and indifference to their plight. These scorned and wretched of the earth- in their desperation to strike out and destroy what they perceived to be the hidden hand of their invisible enemy, attacked not their true enemies; whose purpose it was to keep them oppressed, uneducated, unemployed and illiterate, they struck at those who were most venerable; their brothers and sisters, those who were like themselves who strove to work hard, go to school, and further the interest of themselves and their race. In the ghetto where gangsterism and prison was considered a rite of passage, those who strove to educate themselves were scorned and held in contempt. With great trepidation I speak of these things for in my youth my eyes have beheld many atrocities visited upon my fellow man all in the quest to find one's manhood, all for the purpose of earning respect. In all my years of experience I have never seen one gain manhood or respect through inflicting fear or terror on others. As I look back I do so not in hatred, or judgment, but in understanding. I now know that inner city violence was just a symptom of a larger problem-American violence. A brother by the name of h. Rap brown once said, "Violence was as American as apple pie". Those guilty of perpetuating black on black crime did so only in mock mimicry of their great American forefathers as well as Uncle Sam who gave birth to the America dream through slavery, death, destruction and genocide while maintaining its right to exist through war.

So, I speak from experience, and as an eyewitness, for the things my eyes have beheld are the visions from which nightmares are made of. I was fortunate to survive those times as a lamb walking through the valley of the shadow of death; I use the word fortunate, although many would say I was blessed. Many of my peers and those of my generation were not as lucky as me; they lost their lives from razors, shanks, blunt objects and bullets. Today as in any war-torn segment of the black community, remnants and casualties of these conflicts can be readily seen from those who lay disabled in wheelchairs donning prosthetic limbs and colostomy bags, to those who display amputated limbs, bearing disfiguring scars be it from knives guns or fist, the result is always the same. I repeat I was fortunate for I was blessed not to incur the same assault on my person. I employed the cunning of the fox, the swiftness of the deer and the mind of a strategist. Every move I made was designed to evade those predatory elements of my environment. It was like chess, I made offensive moves to not face capture and be "check mated". The moves I employed in my quest to evade capture gave me the wherewithal to be two steps ahead of those whose desire it was to do me bodily harm. Since my early youth I had to learn two basic rules to the art of war, counterintelligence, and counter insurgency, one's survival and very existence depended on it. I understood thug formations and how to evade them before they formed. I understood the signs, symbols, and language ghetto predators employed before they attacked their prey. In a sense one could say I was blessed with an insight into the mind of the thug, the hard rock, the nigga. This knowledge enabled me to live amongst the beast of the field and dwell in relative safety. Occasionally shit happened on school grounds like fights and robberies, but school was mainly a controlled environment were administrators, school personnel and security could maintain the peace most of the time; outside the school was a different story. At 3:00 o'clock the herd of fresh meat streamed from the school gates on their long but individual journeys toward each of their separate destinations. Some roamed in groups for safety purposes, others -like myself-rolled alone.

I overcame the fears of the high school environment-they were minimal. It was the return home that would become a source of great anxiety to me. It was during this time that I found myself caught up in the throngs of danger that could potentially result in the loss of my life, my property, or my good looks, it was that serious. You had to constantly be on alert and remain vigilant cause if you were caught sleeping you could catch a serious beat down not by just one, but numerous assailants. Mind you these wolfpacks were not composed of mostly teenagers they were composed of grown ass men in their late 20's and early 30's so you wouldn't be getting no school yard ass whipping you would get the type of ass whipping motherfuckers up north were getting, that mature make you bleed, and break bone shit; I've heard the stories and seen the victims. These were dangerous times for young men coming up. During the wilding era a man had to be a man there was no room for sensitive motherfuckers you were either hard rock or pussy there was no in between. The official estimate has never been made but I could say with as surety that during the wilding era an estimated 100,000 black males may have lost their lives during these undeclared ghetto wars. This era marked such a turbulent period in African American history that it was said that if a black man made it to the age of twenty-one, he was considered an OG. In the 80's living was truly about surviving day- to-day by any means necessary, so I took it very seriously. I had to safeguard myself as I traveled to and FRO from school to my home. I usually rode the front of the train because the back of the train is where all the stick-up kids and wolfpacks hunted for prey. I had to be logical, I was only one man, I couldn't fight 20 or 30 motherfuckers, I had hand skills in shit, but it wasn't like I was Bruce lee. Every so often I would throw caution into the wind and ride the back of the train. It was here that I would acquire my hard knocks education.

Wilding was a 3:00 o'clock phenomenon that was more likely to occur during the midday school rush or during the weekend when teenagers were out in the street up to grimy shit. The Deceptigons and the Lo-lives were two crews that were the most infamous during the wilding era, they spread a reign of terror and fear throughout the subway system in every borough of New York's Underground Railroad. These crews used to frequent the a-train the l-train the j-train and the 2 and 3 train, and those who were aware of these thugs' soldiers and their movements made it their business to know how to carefully find ways to avoid them. The Decepts-that's what they were called for short -usually rolled 40 to 50 deep they chose victims at random without cause. It could be how you looked, a stare, what you had on, or your girl, motherfuckers tested your gangster for-anything and if you failed to show and prove, that was enough to get you stomped the fuck out. It was hard being a black man back in the days you couldn't just be you. You had to always walk with a bop and swagger like you was a hard rock nigga. You could never smile in the street, that was against the thug life code of ethics which states: thou shalt not be pussy, if you were guilty of such violations then the ghetto gods of pain might inflict their wrath upon your ass. It was bad enough just being a black man, but it was even worse for pretty boys and light skinned niggas. Back in the days pretty boys had it hard especially light skinned cats. Thugs already hated them for being pretty because they always got all the girls. So pretty boys had it two times harder than the rest of the brothers, they had to act twice as hard and fight ten times as well as the average cat just to get a little respect. I remember this incident that happened one time on the A train with this pretty boy and his girl. They were sitting in the two-seater in the back cart. Generally, the only cats who sat in the back cart were those who packed heat and those who were known thugs.

This pretty boy made the unfortunate mistake of getting caught in the back of train acting to sweet and showing too much of his pearly whites. This nigga was lying on his woman lap while she stroked his head and fed him grapes like a bitch; shit he might as well had suckled the bitch breast. Damn near everybody was looking; even grown ass women, shit just didn't look natural. To most thugs laying in your girl's lap was a straight up bitch move. A platoon of about 35 to 40 Decepts spotted money down the end of the cart. It was too late for duke to man up and put on his game face, niggas saw him pull up his skirt; he was acting pussy. I had my book bag on my lap acting as if I was searching for something as I watched the spectacle unfold. In a way I pitied pretty boy because he knew he was spotted. He sat up and tried to put on a serious thug mug and came off looking like a mix up between al b. Sure and Ricky Richard, it was sad. They sent one of their scouts to test his manhood; it was a cat from Brownsville they used to call powerful. Powerful stepped to duke and ran the bullshit on him, he asked him what size his girls' chain was. Pretty boy's whole expression transformed from a false bravado to a mask of fear. Powerful stepped in front of pretty boy and his girl and propped his polo boots right up on the arm rest and had his dick all in pretty boy's face. He crouched down real close to duke's girl and reached his swelled up calloused black hands towards her chain. He iced grilled duke and cut his eye quickly towards shorty licking his black protruding weed smoking lips. "Excuse me miss I was just admiring your chain, that's that same chain my girl was telling me she wanted. Powerful looked down the end of the cart and gave his peoples the signal that duke was a victim. Just then this short stocky nigga with a red and blue polo rain parka donning a stocking cap vaguely hiding a head full of jail waves burst from the crowd and stepped through the cart swaggering hard with a gait resembling that of a hungry lion. I gazed in sorrow at the hopeless spectacle that was transpiring pretty boy was shook and quiet as a church mouse, he had his head down fearful of gazing into the eyes of his predators. Iron reached out and grabbed shorty chain lifting and weighing its quality in the palm of his hand with the expertise of pawn shop jeweler. Tears began streaming down the face of pretty boy's lady. It was fucked up I

106

instantly empathized with pretty boy and placed myself in his shoes, he had two choices; lunge forward and face a vicious brutal beat down by two stone hearted thugs and lose both his manhood and respect, or do nothing letting his girl, get robbed in front of him and have her lose respect for him; simply put, he was in a no win situation. At that moment both iron and C-God turned their attention to pretty boy they surrounded him on both sides. My girl need that chain, I'm ask you one time, at that moment pretty boy looked up eyes filled with terror for his moment of truth had arrived. Pretty boy was speechless, I felt his pain at that moment I wished I was a magician so that I would have the power to make them both vanish into thin air. C-god and iron both became restless on the part of pretty boys' hesitation to provide them with an answer. Iron knelt over real close to pretty boy close enough to kiss him. Don't let me ask your punk ass again, matter a fact, I aint asking you no more, give me your bitch chain!!! Iron roared as he pushed his hand directly into pretty boy's face mushing his head back so violently that he rammed it to the backwall of seat rest. I watched in shame and disbelief as the victim sat dumbfounded, speechless and frozen with fear for he knew any reply he gave them would result in a serious ass whipping.

At that moment sensing her man had no win's shorty began to loosen the latch of her chain in order to take it off. I watched, everyone watched; no one on the train intervened. Iron was straight gangster he had his hand open to receive his prized merchandise but to my surprised his man laughingly tried to convince iron not to victimize his prey. Chill son let shorty take a walk on that, she can't help it if she got a punk ass man, after she cut duke off maybe the next time, she a find a real man to sport her bad ass. But iron wasn't having it, he paced back and forth like a hungry dog waiting for some scraps. No if she walks somebody going git it regardless, that's word to my four kids. Iron ice grilled money looking for any reason to set it the fuck off, but c-god must have been the ringleader of the crew because iron didn't bust money shit. All right shorty I'm a give you a walk on that cause my man sweet on you, but your man his shit took, git up motherfucker. Pretty boy got up but refused to look his tormentors in the eye. Iron began patting pretty's pockets. All I find all I keep; Iron began to dig his pockets. Pretty boy gave no resistance. That was all iron needed he exploded on pretty boy with a left hook to the temple which blasted Pretty boy's fragile ass head viciously to the left, blood and spit splattered everywhere. He then ended his brutal assault with a right uppercut that broke pretty boys jaw. He instantly crumbled to the floor like a deck of cards and balled up in a tight fetal position. His girl screamed hysterically as iron savagely ripped pretty's pockets money and change splashing everywhere. Pretty lay trembling and sniveling like a virgin who's pussy just got popped. Iron retorted sarcastically next time buy yourself a real man. Iron flicked a crumpled twenty-dollar bill at shorty and swaggered back to his platoon amongst a mist or uproarious shouts of admiration from his thugs' soldiers for his courageous valor on the battlefield. C-God snatched him up and hugged him wildly. He and iron gave each other thunderous pounds, each hand clap resounded like gun fire echoing through the cart. They exited the cart with a roar. I silently prayed for the safety of those innocent souls who would have the misfortune of meeting them. I was spared that day from the wrath of the ghetto gods of pain, I knew one day my time would come. That day I vowed that I would die fighting rather than lose my manhood. Little did I know the gods of destiny heard my vows and were planning to test whether my word was my bond. My trial came quicker than expected, would I be found innocent or guilty, it all depended on me. Would I stand the trial or break under pressure? Would I fold or man up that was the question? My question was answered sooner than expected. I remember well the lesson imparted to me by my mother she always told me as one thinketh so shall it be. After that incident on the train, my mind constantly replayed that fateful event repeatedly. In my mind I replaced pretty boy and shorty was my girl. I pondered one hundred and one ways I might have reacted had I been placed under similar circumstances, and the result remains the same I placed the blame on pretty. It was he who was at fault; had he known the rules of the game he should've rode the front of the train, rode a car to the city, or carried a piece if his hand skills were lacking. The world is a dangerous place and one must always be prepared in order to never get caught sleeping by the predator. I learned how to maneuver on the a-train. After the incident I made it my business never to ride in the rear of the A Train again. All was well for the latter part of 7 months I kicked it with Jose and the rest of my people. Me and Sherina remained good friends-still didn't get no pussy though; but it's all good, I figured the only way I would learn how to relate and understand the female mind was to befriend them and learn their inner secrets.

CHAPTER 13   SUMMERTIME

June was fast approaching I had to keep constantly reminding my mother to get me some gear for the summer. It always seemed as though I was the only one always caught off guard on that first official summer day. Everyone else pulled their freshest gear out the closet and showcased their duds. Players rode down the avenue flamboyantly fronting as the sun shined on their rides which gleamed like diamonds in the sun. The hottest new sounds blared from the Benzes in the back of their trunks. You knew it was summer, the air even smelled different, it was a sweetness in it. As I got older, I later learned that the spring and summer time marked beginnings of the mating season, and that sweet aroma in the air was that of pussy, women, teenagers, and girls, were affected by it as well, it made them excited. They wore tight revealing clothing showcasing every contour of their bodies. They roamed in groups of ten looking for males who were man enough to handle them. Women often played cat and mouse games with men who showed interest, if your game was tight and you were worthy you would get the play. I watched with interest in order to pick up pointers so I could smooth out the kinks in my game. I was young, eager and enthusiastic; I had to learn on my own various aspect of game. But I was a fast learner and I had faith in my skills, but it was the application of game that made me nervous because your delivery had to be correct. Shorty's had to feel your confidence, if they didn't you would know because they would laugh in your face. I was still wet behind the ears and my game was young, but I had to learn fast in order to lay my Mack down in due time. Moms finally gave me enough cash to cop a pair of two-toned acid washed jeans. I was hype because my pants were only fourteen ninety-nine therefore that left me with fifteen dollars in my stash. I ran to "Momo's a clothing shop made famous by the flow of drug dealers who were known to frequent and cop their wares. I brought a white BVD, a silk undershirt that was the hot shit back in the days.

I now had ten dollars; I was doing good. I ran to the barbershop got a fresh fade and kept some hair on top. They used to call this cut the "high low". I had two dollars left. I used my last dollar to cop a pair of fresh socks from the china man on Pitkin Avenue, I now had a dollar left. It was a beautiful summer day and I just let thirty dollars slip through my hand like I had a hole in it, now my pockets were tight I was working with a dollar, but I felt like a million bucks. I was chilling for self I ran to the store brought a twenty-five-cent juice and two bags of chips and took the last quarter and played centipede. Now I had nothing to do, I spent all my money and it was only 11 o'clock. I decided to walk over to my aunt's house and chill with DJ. I slipped through the projects with stealth. Everything I had on was brand new except my sneakers, but if you lived in the ghetto you learned how to hold on to a pair sneaker because you never knew when you would get another pair. I slipped in through the back of 265 Livonia Avenue, the front was usually jammed packed with thugs and drug dealers hustling to get paper. I walked up the narrow stairwell till I reached the fifth floor. My nostrils were assaulted by the smell of incense weed and the stench of poverty. I knocked on the door my aunty opened the door, I gave her a hug and a kiss her on the cheek. I stepped to the back room to check my cousin. The room was immaculate, the beds were made army style, you could bounce a quarter off them, the floors were swept, all my cousins' shoes were perfectly aligned along the wall. DJ was already dressed and ready to go, I was always the slow one, everyone always waited on me, I hated to rush I always felt if I rushed somehow, I was missing something. Yo DJ it's hot as hell outside there's nothing to do, let's get into something.

Everyone had the same thing in mind, going outside, that's when trouble started. Everyone was restless, broke and hot. That was the primary reason in the summertime that most niggas got shot, beat the fuck up, or robbed. The streets weren't safe, you had cats fresh from the penitentiary coming back home trying to muscle in on the drug game. They didn't know the rules, they clashed with the new up and coming knuckle heads and the summers were always filled with bloodshed, but regardless of the fact I didn't give a fuck, confinement wasn't my thing, good times and pussy were on my mind. It was summer and I promised myself that I wouldn't spend it sitting in the house watching Three's company. We were preparing to leave, and my stomach started growling. I knew that a quarter water and bag of chips wouldn't hold me for the day. I ran to the fridge to find some munchies, but all I found was bacon soda and a pitcher of water that smelled like onions. I'm starving, you think Cookie got some money. Shrugging his shoulders, DJ stated, mommy don't never have no money. My mind raced as I thought for a way to solve both our problems. At last I came up with a solution, it was ghetto but when you had lint in your pockets and air in your belly any solution would do. I forgot that the schools all over the area had free lunch programs in the summer, and besides their food was pretty good too. Dee opened the fridge one last time; it was funny how we used to do that, I guess somehow, we figured if we opened it enough food would magically appear there the next time, we peered into it. Seeing that the fridge was bare, dee turned around looked me in the eye gave me the nod, and we bounced. We were on a mission and if it took three, four, or five, schools to satisfy our hunger we were going to hit them we didn't have no shame in our game.

The first spot we hit was PS 284, we were open, when we walked into the entrance security asked us our address; if your address was out of the district you couldn't go to the free lunch in the area, of course I lied and gave an address in the immediate vicinity we gained entry and that was a rap.

Today when I look back on the whole scenario, I see it for what it was-we were poor, we lived in poverty, yet we never knew it, to me the world was a wonderful place filled with adventure. It was only until I grew older and became more conscious of myself, and the world around me, that I realized that as a child I lived like a rat in a maze looking for cheese. Although we lived in poverty, we always found ways to survive because we were innovative, creative and imaginative. We left 284 with full bellies and extra chocolate milks we carefully concealed in our pants. We found a new past time- free lunch hopping. We traveled from school to school from Brownsville to East New York if there was a school we were there. We used to get so much food we began to bring boxes of food home filled with milk, apples, apple sauce, cereal, peanut butter and jelly, and other goodies. My mother used to ask me whether I was heading to the lunch program, cause in a way it softened the economic burden on her back. The Fourth of July weekend was underway, Brownsville day had arrived, and the neighborhood was jumping. In Tilden, Brownsville, Seth low, Langston Hughes, and Vandyke projects people were having sidewalk cookouts, and block parties. Girls from each project used to do cheers; they were dance routines each team used to perform to represent their hoods. Each team used to travel into each other projects to have a dance competition in order ascertain who the best dance team in the neighborhood was. Me and DJ used to follow the dancers from block to block cause most those shorties were hot! I used to like watching them dance nasty, I'm sure a lot of niggas did. Their bodies were muscular and tight and when they danced, they gyrated their pelvic muscles and clicked and bounced every portion of their bodies. I basically fell in love with the summer, she was that girl I used see only once every season, but she warmed my heart and always left me with sweet memories, but see had not yet departed from me so I was going to milk her to the very last.

One thing I particularly liked about the summer was the jams in the park. I remember the music used to be so loud you could hear the pulsating beat from miles and miles away. I remember me and DJ was at my causing Keith's house in East New York, the east was on the other side of the tracks of the 1 train, a lot of niggas used to call this the bridge because you had and elevated train track as well as a freight train track below in a ditch which served as a manmade boundary between East New York and Brownsville. The only way anyone could enter the east was by crossing the bridges that were erected on Pitkin, Sutter, Blake, and Livonia avenues and many a nigga got robbed shot beatdown and killed during their crossing into these enemy territories. Anyway, we heard the music bouncing off the project's walls in Brownsville its vibration and reverberation shook the windows and damn near set off car alarms in the east. Live motherfucker in the east wanted to go but knew they couldn't step to Brownsville projects because they had too much beef with certain niggas but the beauty about me and DJ, we had ghetto passes, we could freely travel from East New York to Brownsville without being stepped to because we had family in the east, and niggas just knew our faces, we were cool like that. It was a warm summer night and excitement was in the air we travel over the Blake avenue bridge and headed down Blake towards the Brownsville houses, it was as if the music had an aroma but instead of its sweet scent carrying us by our nostrils towards our destination the sweet sound of the music carried our bodies. As we grew closer, we knew we were at the right place cause you saw down by law type chicks draped in the hottest gear heading towards Brownsville's heart. That was the funny thing about Brownsville houses its court yards were smack dab in the middle of the residential grounds, with its buildings carefully surrounding and concealing it, so if you were and outsider and you didn't know your way around you might consider the "yard" a death trap; for many it was.

It was about 10:30 at night, we knew basically that our asses were supposed to be in the house, but the lure of the jam was too much for us to contend with. The music, the bass, the smiles on niggas faces expressed more words than any could convey. We stepped down the walkway of the narrow enclosure leading to the courtyard on eastern side of Brownsville project complex. The magic had already started, brothers had shorties hemmed up in dark corners tonguing them down; shit was getting heavy. You saw niggas running their hands up and down shorty's bodies, some of them had their hands in girls' pants. As we neared the entrance to the yard, all you heard was the sound of people partying. The bass from the speakers was earth shattering, it shook your clothes. The DJ was bumping that shit "milk dee" and everyone in the yard danced in unison, all you saw were oceans of people freaking it; it was mind blowing. This was the first jam I ever attended and every one was doing their thing, girls danced with guys and older people did their two step, even thugs held their own, that was a sight to behold watching the hardest niggas do their warrior dances as they swaggered holding their forties ounces high for all the world to see, it was shocking to me because I never knew thugs could dance. We viewed the spectacle in awe as we chilled near the speakers, it was like we were in another world for once it seemed black people had achieved a sort of unity, they were held together by the music. I guess I must have spoken to soon because at that moment I saw some cat from East New York looking chinky eyed from smoking weed drinking a forty next to the DJ square. I wasn't the only one who spotted him, niggas from Langston Hughes had their eyes on duke from the moment he stepped in the yard. They must have run back to get the mob squad because they were rolling mad deep the next time, I saw them.

Me and dee knew shit was about to jump off- it was in the air. Others may have been oblivious to it to the danger at hand but me and DJ had nigga radar, and our senses told us to keep one foot at the ready cause if the shit hit the fan, I didn't want to get any on my ass, if you know what I mean. This nigga from the east must have been strapped, either that, or he just had mad heart, because he was chilling hard nursing a forty-ounce moving back and forth to the music, not giving a fuck. I peeped the whole scene unfolding. In about two minutes ten hard rocks with hoodies converged on his position. They all formed a line -one in front of the other, they then held on to one another and viscously rushed through the crowd knocking everyone to the side roaring in unison: Brownsville, never ran never will, Brownsville, never ran, never will, outsiders get rushed and get killed! They all began to spread out in the crowd dancing while holding bats in their hands; that was a bad sign. They all began to form a loosely cropped circle around the victim. One by one thugs began to test money armor they walked past him playing him mad close looking him fiercely in his grill some bumped him while others stepped past him and uttering obscenities in his face. Me and DJ felt sorry for duke because we realized that this nigga was high, and since his reaction time was mad slow, he was just realizing what the fuck was about to go down. All the lights were out in the courtyard so all you saw was the flicker of lighters and the lighted butts of cigarettes and herb. Suddenly in a flash they pounced on him like a pack of hungry wolves; all you heard was the sound of knuckles hitting raw flesh. He tried run, all to no avail. This kid ran up on him and cracked him in the head with a bat. Blood spurted from his wound like water and he emitted a high pitch scream as he scrambled to escape. Like a wounded animal he ran sideways in a daze holding the side of his head. Everyone began to scream and run, they stampeded out of the courtyard like a herd of wild buffalo and ran in every direction to escape the carnage. Duke regained his composure, crouched down and pulled a 22 caliber out his sock. In a blind fury he began shooting indiscriminately into the crowd, at that moment me and DJ started jetting in the opposite direction we had already mapped out our route of escape before the chaos ensued, and one thing me and DJ knew how to do was run. As we exited Brownsville houses, we ran across mother Gaston Blvd. As soon as we were in Vandyke projects all you heard was the sound of gunfire. Jams in the park were the highlight of the summer months but it was the violence that brought them to an end. To many niggas had beef, too many niggas had weapons; and too many niggas just didn't give a fuck. In the beginning jams were used to celebrate our communities' culture, but within the last few years before its eventual demise jams began to attract all the wrong elements. Thugs, gangs, hoodlums, and stickup kids became the order of the day. No longer could children make up creative dances and have contest celebrating and representing their projects, the jams became war zones in which rivals played out and settled their petty beefs. Bloodshed gang violence and death became the norm. It was the mid-eighties and what little quality of life we enjoyed in our neighborhood was on the decline. The ghetto was in its death throws. The drug trade was beginning to flourish, the decent working-class families who took pride in the neighborhood were leaving in droves and the remnant of ghetto folks who were unemployed, underemployed, or on welfare, would be the spark responsible for igniting the crack cocaine epidemic.

Fortunately for me I was blessed with mother intuition, I knew Brownsville was increasingly becoming a danger zone, so I found other areas to play in, namely East New York. I used to chill with my cousin Keith and Walter. Me, DJ, Keith, and Horney, used to hang out in Blake and Williams avenue. We found shit to do, we were very creative that way. When most cats just stood in front of the building doing nothing, we used to go through Keith's house open the window and climb on the fire escape and belt out some smooth tunes from new edition to girls we saw passing on the streets below. We were pretty good too. On days when you could see the heat rising from the pavement and the tar in the streets seemed to melt, we all used to leave East New York and travel over the notorious Livonia avenue bridge and go to Betsy Head swimming pool. Now you talking about a thug paradise, that was the spot! If you wanted to keep your clothes your best bet was to never place them in the gym lockers. Cats used to sneak in the locker rooms with lock cutters and steal niggas sneakers, shirts, money or whatever valuable possessions they had that was worth shit. Betsy hay was composed of two pools one sixteen-footer that lied at the eastern portion of the pool. And the five-footer, that was the larger of the two and covered three fourths of the pool inner perimeter. The sixteen feet had a very ominous history, it was said that over fifteen people had drowned in the pool since its opening; many believed that the pool was haunted. The sixteen feet was for professional swimmers. Mostly the lifeguards used to frequent the area near the diving board rapping to chicks who was riding the dick. But the Betsy head pool was mainly for motherfuckers who wanted to show off their jail muscles. The hard rocks used to come to the pool to rob people and get shorties. Me, DJ, and Keith used to come to the pool to watch ass, and pussy, that was our sole motivation.

The pool usually opened in July around independence weekend, but most if not all of Brownsville notorious elite, the hard rocks, stickup kids, hoodlums, and way ward kids, usually found ways to beat the feverish heat of the concrete ghetto jungles. We used to sneak in the pool late at night. The moon light parties in the pool used to be the shit back in the days. Kids used to get a wire cutter and clip open the wire mesh gate and everybody used to sneak in the side of the pool with their radios their girlfriends and their weed, you would think it was club med for niggas in shit. Most of the time me, DJ, and Keith, would go to the midnight parties just to cool off and swim a bit, but others came to Betsy Head to have sex in the pool. I was a nasty little dude when I was young. Me and DJ used to watch niggas and bitches fucking in the water. There were two lighthouse towers jutting out of the water in the middle of Betsy head's large pool area; couples often used this as a staging area for their sexual escapades. We used to watch couples fuck up against the tower walls. You saw five and six couples just bobbing up and down; some shorties were strapped around their man's waist riding the dick. You could see girls their faces were rammed against the wall of the light house while their man straddled them from behind, you just knew they were getting their back blown out "doggy style". The beautiful thing about it all was we never got caught, there was always a lookout stationed at the gate to warn us if the cops were coming. I always looked forward to the summer, it was a time that always left me with numerous memories. The summer was even reflected in the music, you could hear a song and start reminiscing on your first love, your first kiss or your first crush. It was the sights, sounds, and smells of summer that made it so special. The barbeques, the dance contest, the block parties, and hot summer nights where everyone just hung out to the wee morning hours made it the season I looked forward to with anticipation.

CHAPTER 14   NEW LOTS AVE

The spirit of adventure roared through my heart back in those days. I wanted to explore my entire word and beyond. I was young, black, and I felt invincible. The summertime provided me with the release I needed to suspend all this pent-up energy. My cousin and I ran the streets like we didn't have a home. When we wore out all the hang out spots in Brownsville, ran through all our hideouts in East New York, we were once again on the move in search of adventure. We used to creep to the other side of town where there were other sorts of fun of a more nefarious kind. Soon enough we found just what we were in search of. We began hanging out with my cousins Ephraim and Cleveland who used to come to Brooklyn every summer to hang on new lots avenue with their aunt Millie, that's when we got put on to that side. New Lots Avenue was a grimy stretch of road which had its beginning at the intersection of Mother Gaston Blvd. in front of lot avenue projects and ended at Fountain Avenue in front of the entrance to the notorious cypress hill projects. Since the 40's New Lots Avenue served as a haven for blacks arriving from the southern states in search of better opportunities. Composed mainly of row houses by the mid-seventies with the loss of Brooklyn's factory economy new lots avenue quickly degenerated into a ghetto of the most pernicious type. By the 1980's 95% of the neighborhood was comprised of welfare recipients, drug addicts, the homeless, the working-class poor, Hispanics, and the newly arrived West Indian population. With this social cultural dynamic in place the stage was ripe for the explosion of the emerging drug trade. Since the disease of poverty preyed upon the mind's bodies and souls of the poor, crack would be used by the drug dealer as the magic elixir to cure the suffering of their wretched lot. Seizing the opportunity to expand on the new flourishing drug trade, the Rastas quickly took control of the crack trade and held New Lots in a grip of iron.

Traveling from Blake and Williams down Hinsdale Avenue towards New Lots was like traversing through a war zone. Every block ventured through was filled with abandoned dilapidated buildings covered with vegetation. Packs of diseased festered dogs roamed in packs of ten. The smell of death and decay assaulted the nostrils; you could smell dead animals in various stages of decomposition. Water always ran from rusted fire hydrants in these ghetto wastelands. The fire hydrant was the ghetto watering hole. Man, and beast alike lapped up water from these spouts to quench their thirst. Men long forgotten by the society congregated in packs, some sat on discarded couches, others on milkcrates. As I gazed upon their faces, which sometimes I did, I saw in them a sense of deep hopelessness. I saw men who no longer cared whether they lived or died, men to whom hardship and suffering became an intimate friend. Their stories were etched deeply into their emotionless faces. Each told the same story of wanting to live the American dream, a dream only allotted to the privileged few, those whose white skins and ivy league educations allowed them to receive the red carpet treatment, not those whose mothers and fathers picked cotton and were sharecroppers only one generation removed from slavery; theirs was the story of a dream deferred. Nevertheless, me and DJ crept through this desolate landscape till we arrived at our new hang out spot which looked more like a refugee camp if you ask me. We always got mad love from our peoples once we hit the block. It was our ritual to give each other extended soul pounds and play box with each other as we extended our greetings. Our cousin Ephraim; back in day we used to call him easy-e, he used to come from far as far-rockaway to Brooklyn with his brother Cleveland to get into a little something during summertime. As young adolescents we always had fun because we were a diverse group of individuals. We all had our own personalities and our own way of doing things, there was never a clash of personalities. Cleveland was into the martial arts, he was bugged out, he used to come all the way from far-rockaway with Chinese slippers on karate pants and no shirt; everybody used to call him nature boy. Ephraim was totally the opposite. He was obsessed with wrestling. He would watch wrestling matches on television and master most of their moves which he would later use in the streets. My cousin DJ also was obsessed with the martial arts. Bruce lee was his idol and he was able to mimic move for move every technique Bruce Lee was famous for. He also had mastery over the nun-chucks. I guess all of us gravitated towards martial discipline in one way or the other. It was all the testosterone flowing through our veins as we went through the transition from adolescence to manhood. I my self was very into all this macho man shit, I was trying to define my manhood, trying to find myself. I was into war movies boxing and almost anything involving combat. It was our differences that complemented each other and brought us together, little did we know that it was these differences that would help mold us into a click, a crew, a posse, but more on that later. Millie, Ephraim and Cleveland's aunt, used to hang with two chickens' heads named Sharon and iris. Sharon was a homely motherfucker who lived on the second floor in the building. She had a whole bunch of dusty looking brothers and sisters who looked like they hadn't bathed or eaten in days. Their house was unkempt, there was clothes lying in heaps in each corner of the room, a million unwashed plates on the dining table and the sink was filled to the brim with dirty water because the drain was clogged with god knows what. The bedroom had old pissy dirty mattresses lying on the floor with piss stained bedspreads covering them. All the windows in the crib were slightly cracked and had clear plastic bags covered the windowpanes. The bathroom was disgusting; the toilet was always congested with shit cause the pipes were always backed up. The bathtub was filled with black putrid water and heaps of filthy clothes that had not been washed in ages, and on top of that the house was infested with rats, roaches water bugs and mice. Why did we hang out there; we hung out there because we could do any fucking thing we wanted to do-and that we did.

We came to New Lots and sat in front of the building and bugged out with iris, Millie, Sharon, Ephraim and Cleveland. We sometime broke day. It wasn't that we were smoking weed, or drinking liquor; I hadn't reached that phase yet. I used to get a natural high just hanging out, talking shit laughing and joking with my peoples. That was enough to make it all worthwhile. But believe you me it was a lot of perks involved with hanging with Sharon in them on New Lots Avenue. I may have not realized it at the time, but we were the liveliest motherfuckers on the avenue and lots of people stood up and took notice. Everybody began hanging in front of Sharon's building, it became like a big party. I wasn't mad either, a lot of new opportunities to meet bitches and get pussy began to open for us. The nature of the game began to radically change when niggas started to get pussy. There were three chicks that had a profound effect on our crew. There was Rhonda, she was a Puerto Rican cutie who started hanging around with us on Sharon's block after shit started to get live. Rhonda was mollies and iris friend. Me, DJ, Cleveland and Ephraim were strung out on Rhonda. We all were jostling for position to get in them draws. We all had what we believed to be the method; the rap formula to bag up cuties, but we were still young, dumb and trying to get some. Then there was Donna, Ephraim used to talk to her, but she was a young hoe in training, she was everyone's girl. Then there was Shawn; Shawn was mollies friend, and she was short pretty and chocolate with a fat ass and round tities. She always asking about DJ when he wasn't around-lucky nigga. I wasn't involved with anyone I wanted to mess with them all. One night me, DJ, Cleveland Ephraim, Millie, Sharon, iris and Rhonda, sat in front of the building drinking quarter waters eating chips and talking about everybody who walked past our doorstep. Millie noticed Cleveland staring deeply at Rhonda's caramel complexioned legs, thighs, and ass as she sat on the milk crate. Millie, peeped Cleveland clocking Rhonda and seized the chance to put Cleveland on the spot. She couldn't help it Sharon, and iris had a penchant for gossiping and instigating shit as well.

126

They always wanted to know the scoop on everything and everyone; we used to call them the three musketeers. Millie put Cleveland on the spot like a motherfucker and called him out in front of everybody. "Cleveland you think you slick, I see you staring at Rhonda, you like Rhonda don't you ". Cleveland looked like a cornered animal trying to find a means of escape, his eyes darted in every direction in frantic desperation. He was trying to think of a way to deflect attention from himself without looking like a sucker. All eyes were on him and we all waited for a reply. He answered the only way he could he shuddered and couldn't speak and gazed directly at the floor. he could no longer peek at the object of his desire because his secret lust for her was no longer a secret. Rhonda smiled and was flattered. Rhonda you feeling my nephew, let me find out, Millie gushed. She then pushed Cleveland towards Rhonda and badgered Rhonda till she got next to him. Cleveland looked in our direction. Me, Ephraim, and DJ gave him the nod of approval all the while moving our heads frantically to the left telling him with the flaring of our eyes to step up and bag her. As he moved towards her, at that moment everybody began hyping shit up making what initially was an awkward situation even worse. You the man, cried DJ. Cleveland smiled and stuck his tongue out in a bashful yet playful manner. "That's my baby bro', Ephraim gave Cleveland a slap on the back and a pound as he waltzed pass him with Rhonda. I just smiled a knowing smile and hoped in my heart that Cleveland had game enough to pull Rhonda because she was a bonafide dime.

Cleveland must have had enough game to pull his prize because from that day forward he and Rhonda became an item. Yet unbeknownst to us this would be the beginning of hell on earth for her as Cleveland began his spiral down the path of destruction-but that's another story. After Cleveland and Rhonda got together, Donna came into the picture. Donna was Shawn's friend, she used to come around on the weekends and bug out with us. You could just look at her and know she was nasty. She wasn't ugly or nothing; actually, she was pretty, but she had a wide ass smile that stretched from ear to ear with these big dick sucking lips. She had large almond shaped eyes, the type of eyes that would look through you if you were fucking her. She had a devilish sort of innocence that attracted us all. She was a big flirt. There was a game we used to play in the dark vestibule of Sharon's building. Me, DJ, Ephraim, Sharon, Donna, and sometimes even Cleveland, we used to go into the hallway, lock the door, cut out the lights, and play the kissy felly game. The object of the game for the guys was just to squeeze, hump, and kiss, as much ass, titties, and pussy, as possible before the lights got turned on without getting caught. It was a free for all. Sharon and them would act like they were fighting us off, but they would let us get our rub and hump on. That's when I found out just how nasty Donna really was. On one occasion I got the opportunity to ger her alone in the vestibule when I left Sharon's house on my way to the store. She followed me into the dark hallway and started rubbing my dick. I was young and this shit didn't happen to me on the regular, this was a new experience. Back in the days it was unheard of for a woman to push up and try to Mack a nigga, so naturally my first reaction was to pull back from her and move her hand. I'll admit she had me kind of shook, I didn't know how to handle her approach, but I'd be damned if I was going to let this chick punk me. I moved her hand off my dick and pushed her up against the was pulling both her hands behind her back. I was aggressive but I had to show her that I was a fucking man. I pressed up on her hard and started tongue kissing her forcefully.

She responded to my overtures by wrapping her hands around me gripping my ass with so much force her nails bit into my flesh; this bitch was into some bullshit. It was hurting like hell, but I didn't want to cry out, so I held the pain and continued to kiss her, she ten grabbed me around my neck and wrapped both her legs around my waist straddling me; shorty was on some shit. She began thrusting her tongue deeply down my throat to the point where I almost gasped. I was about to pull back when she clamped down on my lip with her teeth and bit the shit out of me. I had enough, I shoved her with all my might, and she fell back against the wall. This bitch was crazy, she stared at me as if she was truly enjoying the spectacle of this shit. Is this what you want nigga, she rubbed the crotch of her pussy and looked at me defiantly. Donna then rushed towards me and grabbed my dick once more, this time she did it with so much force that spams of pain shot through my body. I winced in pain and viscously jerked away from her. I knew you was scared, she said with a devilish look her eyes. You can't handle me nigga! I looked at her with disgust and retorted, if that's all you have to offer, I don't want it. I think Donna was genuinely intrigued by me from that point on. We both stood in the dark vestibule heaving form exhaustion after our sick escapade. I felt a mixture of revulsion and lust; I was only sixteen and had never experienced no sadomasochist shit before. I had never told anyone what really happened that day, I lied telling them that we had got our kiss, rub, and flirt on. Eventually everybody got a chance to get Donna in the hallway at Sharon's house, but my cousin Ephraim after he got his rub on, he turned donna into his girl. That's where he fucked up, how could he expect the crew to have respect for his shorty after everybody done humped, squeezed, and kissed all over this chick. I guess he was the only one who got open and caught feelings; eventually Ephraim had to find out the hard way. One day me, DJ, Shawn, Cleveland, Rhonda, Ephraim and donna went uptown to catch a movie on 42nd street. We went to catch the three for five specials; you couldn't beat that. Three karate flicks for five dollars- that's what up. Back in the day you didn't really have to buy food from the movies and shit, everybody just brown bagged it; they brought forties weed and sometimes twenty-two's in brown bags. We all bought our popcorn, candy and soda, from the store, and had them packed away in our bookbags. We slid into the theater three minutes before the movie was about to begin. We caught the intermission. They were always showing some dumb shit during the intermission about dancing candies and shit; I never paid much attention to it. You knew the movie was about to begin because as the lights began to dim, the cigarettes and the weed began to blaze hazing up the whole movie house. To see the torch of a dozen cigarettes glowing luminescent through tobacco fog was kind of exotic in an odd sort of way. Everyone came to the movies for a variety of different reasons. Some came to fuck; the theater was built for that shit. The top row in the corner was usually the darkest spot in the house. Couples who wanted to fuck usually frequented that area to carry out those intentions. Others came to the movies with crews 50 to

130

100 men strong, they were there to start trouble, they wanted to fight, cut, rob and stick motherfuckers up for their jewelry, money, sneakers, or whatever. Some unfortunate souls got their ass whipped just on general principle alone. I came to the movies just to be with my peoples and have fun, little did I know I would be here to get some stinky finger.

We all shuffled together and sat in one row. I sat at the end of the row facing the isle; Donna sat her flat ass next to me. Ephraim sat next to her, DJ and Shawn cuddled next to each other, and Cleveland and Rhonda sat in front row.

He always did something to stand out from the crowd. As the lights dimmed, the room became enveloped in a curtain of pure darkness. My body was tensed and arched forward because I had become so engrossed in this action pact movie. The audience wailed as the intensity of the movie began to escalate. The tumult of noise became deafening as groups of rowdy hard rock niggas began to act the fool standing up on chairs, swinging their fist, shadow boxing at the screen mimicking their approval. I didn't move a muscle; I was entranced peering intently at each kung Fu technique in a bid to learn some techniques through osmosis. Suddenly, the quite reflection of my world shattered, the focus of my attention had been broken. I no longer gazed upward at the reflection of the screen; my eyes shot downward 45 degrees. Peering through the piercing darkness at what appeared to be a hand on my crotch. Was this chick for real? Donna was stroking my dick while she sat next to my man Ephraim. If I screamed on Donna and immediately told Ephraim what had just transpired, he might turn on me calling me a liar accusing me of being jealous of his relationship. On the other hand, I knew DJ knew, and

Cleveland knew she was a hoe; hell, even she knew, so I might as well enjoy the shit and keep it on the low I reasoned. It was kind of foul but fuck it. He'd probably do it to me if given a chance. My mind was made up, I laid back and relaxed resigned to the fact that I might as well get mines.

Donna wasn't new at this shit, she was an expert, adept at covert cock stroking. I couldn't believe her nerve; my cousin, Ephraim her man sitting right beside her, and yet this bitch was able to unzip my zipper with her left hand and finagle the slit in my boxer shorts so that the helmet of my dick reared its mighty head form hiding. Looking straight ahead, beads of sweat began to form at my brow and trickled freely down the bridge of my nose as I experienced ecstatic explosions of ecstasy as her fingers worked their magic. Peering from my left eye nervously I noticed Ephraim, who seemed totally oblivious to the spectacle that was occurring. This was some real taboo freaky shit. At that time, I knew nothing about how the fear of getting caught could heighten one's sexual pleasure, but as her baby smooth-yet sensual hand stroked up and down back and forth along the shaft of my cock I felt I was about to explode. Never had my dick been this hard, never had I ever been this excited. My heart pulsed rapidly; my blood boiled. My cock became so erect it seemed as if it had a mind of its own. It bobbed up and down, pulsing rhythmically to the beat of my heart. At that moment I was in the zone, I didn't give a damn whether I got caught or not; I was two seconds from nutting in my pants. The reality struck me like a bolt of lightning. A wave of guilt swept over me like a tsunami. I was a foul ass nigga and this was some foul ass shit. All my cousin had to do was look over at me and I would be cold busted with my dick in her hand; all this for a nut, it wasn't worth it, I reasoned. Peering sensually into Donnas eyes I shook my head reluctantly signifying that this mischief had to come to an end. Donna purred devilishly and began stroking my cock even faster. I began to lose control, my eyes rolled to the back of my head, I was about to come. And she was determined to see me climax, however she would not be the victor of this escapade. At that moment I firmly grasped her right hand prying it away from my throbbing dick which had already the telltale signs of orgasm; translucent droplets of pre-cum gathered at the head of my dick in anticipation for ejaculation. Luckily for me the tumult of the raucous audience and the smell of weed, wine and cigarettes muffled the sound of my moaning and the smell of hot sex in the air. Seemingly undeterred, moving like a hungry predator, Donna, her eyes reflecting like a beast of prey grimaced wickedly. She wouldn't take no for an answer, if she couldn't get me off, she would make damn sure that she got off. A dense fog of weed enveloped the theater. Hard rocks, thugs and stickup kids, roared in unison as the kung-Fu flick reached a crescendo of mindless violence. However, I was engaged in a battle of my own, and I was losing. Donna was not yet finished with me. She crossed her legs exposing the crotch of her panties as her warm soft honey brown caramel thighs seductively called me. She beckoned me with her eyes to touch her forbidden fruit. Her eyes spoke to me; and reach for her I did. My hands trembled, my body shook, my mouth became as dry as a desert as my hand explored the expanse of her sweet young flesh. Stroking her thighs my hand traveled up her powerfully built legs ending at the soft fold of her ass. She wore sheer pantyhose -coffee brown which

133

accented her legs like silk drapes on a canopy. My dick throbbed painfully, it wanted to poke some pussy, however my fingers would be the only one doing the fucking tonight. My hand disappeared between her dark hued thighs. I stroked, caressed and fondled the crotch of her pussy until the slippery dew of her vagina soaked the fabric of her panties and her stockings. Donna moaned and wiggled sensually as my four fingers explored her labia and her clitoris. Emboldened, I hungered for more. I wanted to feel the real thing, I wanted to plunge my fingers deep into her hot pussy. Donna arched her back and hiked her crossed legs even further allowing me to play with her hot box. She moaned and clenched her teeth. This shit was surreal, it was like some pornographic fantasy. I couldn't believe I was doing this shit. Tearing a small nape in Donna stocking, I inserted my finger and began to rip a hole the size of my hand in to her pantyhose. The satin was soft to my touch as I gripped the elastic sheath covering her moist vagina. Pulling her panties aside, I delved my fingers into her hot box and began massaging her vaginal walls in a circular motion. Donna she handled my technique like a pro, she began tightening her pussy muscles on my finger. Sweat ran down my underarms and my back as though I were fully engaged in intercourse with this chick. I was new to this foreplay shit, I was young, dumb and trying to get some. I was used to sticking and moving, I was a dog in training and Donna was grooming me to be a young p-l-m-p. My cock was red hot and rock hard for too damn long and I wasn't getting my dick wet, it began to become painful. At that time, I had never experienced blue balls, that was a phenomenon outside my limited sexual experience, but I was soon to learn the hard way that karma was truly a bitch.

On the return home I cried like a bitch. I was curled in a fetal positon like a newborn babe fresh out the pussy. My balls felt as if they were withdrawing into my stomach, the pain was excruciating. I often wondered what menstrual cramps felt like; I guess this was my way of experiencing the pain firsthand from a male perspective. I guess this was Gods way of smiting me for my betrayal. That night everyone believed that I suffered from an upset stomach; only me Donna and god would ever know the truth.

I learned many critical lessons that summer. One: I still had much to learn about women. Two: everything that looks good is not good for you. Although a cherry may look sweet if eaten before its ripe it could poison you. I pondered that women of all shapes and sizes were beautiful sexy alluring creatures, but like the lioness if you stroked them the wrong way you could get bitten. The summer came and went like the rising and setting of the sun. I grew older, colder, and wiser as the hands of time slowly progressed. Life was hard and vicious, if you were to slow at mastering its lessons it would eat your ass up and spit or shit you out. I studied the game and learned it well. I began to understand that the older a mother fucker became the more the game became about money and fame. In order to Mack chicks you had to have bricks, in order to get ass, you had to have cash. In contrast the broke mother fucker always got played like a sucker. Although I understood the base fundamentals of being a player a Mack and a pimp, I was missing one key element, I didn't have cash in my stash, that's what kept me messed up and out of luck.

CHAPTER 15   ENTERING THE GAME

It was 1985 at the height of the crack cocaine epidemic. Everybody who was somebody was a player in the drug game. If you weren't pushing a Volvo, a Saab, BMW or Mercedes, heavy on the jewels, rocking gold fronts furry angels, Bally's, Rolex watches and carrying a mint of cash on the daily, fly bitches wasn't fucking with you-bottom line family! We hung on New Lots where niggas and Rastas was getting "pasta" (money), where niggas who knew how to bake was making cake. I was a young nigga striving to be fly, damn right I wanted a piece of the pie. However, I understood that life was about choices; that was one of the many lessons my mother conveyed to me as a young man. She would tell me that life involved cause and effect, action and reaction. For every good or bad act there followed consequences. As a result, one would either suffer positive or negative karma (fate). My mother taught me that those who lived by the sword inevitably would die by the sword.

I was instilled with a strong sense of morals and values. I knew if I strayed to the dark side and began to delve into a life of fast money, cars, hoes and clothes that my punishment would be seven times as severe because I knew better, I knew right from wrong. The drug game was highly lucrative but had a high turnover rate. So many young black men-potential doctors, lawyers, scientist, husbands, fathers, grandfathers, uncles and sons had been lured down the path to destruction by the illusion of wealth and power that accompanied being involved in the drug game. So many lost their lives, so many lost their freedom for the promise of wealth; crack was the white piped piper that led hundreds of thousands down the path to destruction. Thousands of families were destroyed. Mothers who were the backbone of their families got sucked into the cycle of chemical warfare and genocide that crack visited upon the African American community. Many became crack addicts and sold their ass for next to nothing for the promised of securing the next hit. Many fell so low that they sold their bodies for fifty cents or a dollar to get enough change to cop a small vial of crack. While others committed atrocities against their own family by pimping out their own daughters for crack. Their children were used as collateral in exchange to purchase crack on credit-shit was diabolical. Their innocence was lost; like cattle they were bartered, bought, sold, used, abused and then discarded.

I had to make a choice; would I give in to my desire for material possessions and all the so-called perks accompanying it; the fame the fortune, money, power and respect, or would I be disciplined staving off my desire for material items in order to live an ethical life of hard work and moral turpitude as my mother and others had done. Fuck that is wanted pussy, fly bitches, fame and shorty's; I had one life to live I reasoned, and I would live my life to the fullest. Shit pussy was a commodity to be bought and sold. Those who had the dough brought the hoes and the hoes sold their wares to the highest bidder. Just like any other drug pussy involved supply and demand. Fly chicks were in short supply and choice pussy was in high demand. Only the freshest playas, the ballers, the dons and the big willies could compete amongst each other on a level playing field. Those who were not in the game couldn't compete at all, unfortunately, I was one of them.

My cousin Cleveland was one of those who made the choice early in the game. He joined this nefarious fraternity of hustlers, ballers and players who were in to win it. He joined the life because he felt he had to, he was fucking with Rhonda, the only Puerto Rican dime piece on New Lots Avenue. Getting cash by any means necessary was the only aim to achieve one's fame, and Cleveland wasn't about to get played by the next man.

At a time when black men were faced with the choice of abject poverty or achieving the prospect of rags to riches overnight many chose the latter, Cleveland was one of them. No longer satisfied with lamenting about how other cats where getting money. Cleveland started drug running for this cat named iron on New Lots and Sheffield. Iron was the biggest drug dealer in east New York. Cleveland started out modestly. Like any other job a motherfucker had to earn a certain amount of trust, so iron placed Cleveland on probation until he proved his worth. He started off as a look out, he was responsible for warning iron's drug soldiers and army of workers if the police were casing his drug territories in a bid to raid his operation, the money was sweet. He earned $100.00 a day-straight cash. There was also perks involved; all the weed you could smoke and all the pussy you could fuck; drug dealers had groupies too. Although Cleveland worked 12 hours a day, by the end of the week he earned a cool $700 dollars tax free. He was on his way up the ladder-or so we thought. After a few months Cleveland started wearing Rolex watches, rope chains, Kangal hats, silks shirts, wallaby Clarks, and donned rings on every finger. He and Rhonda began wearing matching velour suits and sneakers and Cleveland carried a mint of cash-over 2g's every day. We all began to look up to Cleveland. He quickly rose the drug ranks from a lookout, to a carrier, to a bag man in little over a year. Cleveland was now one of iron's pristine lieutenants in his intimate circle. Cleveland was now earning no less than $500.00 dollars a week and became a man of respect renown and power. Gone were the days when like us he cried about being broke and not having enough money to buy a bag of chips, now he was the man, who was fast becoming a baller and shot caller.

The money was lovely, and Cleveland got caught up in the game. He no longer hung with our crew, he was hanging out with Jamaican cats and mimicked their style, dance, fashion and swag. He now hung exclusively with iron and his Rastafarian posse; in addition, he also adopted a Jamaican accent to fit his new persona. He was now the envy of his friends' peers and associates. Cleveland had gained a volatile reputation for his warrior's prowess and his take no shit attitude. He was a man of action, skilled in the art ninjutsu; he put his skills to good use. He became one of irons hench men. If any worker came up short on cash or drug loot Cleveland was employed to set an example. He broke cats' arms, legs, fingers and collarbones. He shattered jaws and knocked mother fuckers' teeth the fuck out; and the scary thing was he enjoyed it.

Although Cleveland was now known throughout East New York, to us he was still Cleveland. We grew up together; in our eyes he was not this infamous drug soldier that brought fear by the mere mention of his name. But indeed, shit was changing, Cleveland started acting differently. He was in a different circle now and he had to maintain his reputation by any means. Any show of kindness was an indication of a weakness, a weakness that his enemies could exploit. He could not afford this at this level of the game; he would employ everything he learned previously as a member of the guardian angels to charm, deceive, maneuver and manipulate those who were fast becoming his enemies. Cleveland was not only well versed at the physical side of the martial arts; he was also versed in the mental aspect of ninjutsu. He learned that only by remaining close to one's enemies could one gain a true understanding of how they thought. He knew certain workers in his inner circle hated him. They were becoming envious of his fame, although he wasn't bigger than iron, Cleveland was on the come up, quiet as kept, the streets were talking. Cleveland had now rose to a level in his infamous career where he knew the time was ripe for him to branch out and start his own shit. However, he couldn't rely on iron's workers to help him re-up and expand his new operations; they couldn't be trusted. Cleveland knew if he put these mother fuckers on, they would destroy his shit from within, these niggas were haters, and if they tried to skim off the top and steal his shit, he would have to peel back one of their caps. With no one left to trust, Cleveland became paranoid. He began to carry around an arsenal of weaponry. He carried a 45-millimeter German Luger, a sawed off shot gun and a snub nose 38 special with the shock absorbing grip. Although he was proficient in the martial arts Cleveland wanted to be prepared just in case a mother fucker ran up on him and tried to pop his ass, better to be safe than sorry he reasoned.

With word on the grape vine that Cleveland had aspirations of becoming a drug king, iron now began distrusting Cleveland. Where previously iron gave Cleveland free rein over many of his drugs spots now, he had Cleveland teamed up with one of his flunkies in order to ensure he was not scheming to initiate a hostile takeover. To add insult to injury iron began to limit the hours Cleveland worked in the drug spot. Cleveland profits began to plummet; iron hit Cleveland where it hurt the most; in his pockets.

Enough was enough, Cleveland wasn't going to let no fucking body, play him like he was a new jack sucker, he had big plans. Yes! He was going to go into business for himself. Yes! He was going to be a motherfucking don-dada, and yes, he was planning to beat iron at his own game; but little did we know his plans involved us.

After returning from the spot Cleveland came to DJ's house mad as a hell. He paced back and forth as though he were a caged animal and brooded as though he were a man possessed with thoughts of mayhem and murder. DJ's house was usually the meeting place for members of the crew because Aunty Cookie worked the night so that was our time to get into all kind of mischief. Me, DJ, Keith, and Ephraim had spent the night that evening when Cleveland called the house and told DJ he was coming over; he sounded hyped agitated and out of breath, and hurriedly resounded that he had some shit to tell us. My stomach felt fucked up, something was wrong, fear had a way setting off my biological alarm system; it was sort of my own personal Spidey sense.

When he arrived, his eyes were bloodshot red, and he reeked of weed and Hennessey. Looking around as though he were casing the joint, he asked, is cookie here. He entered the crib and began to unload all his weaponry and place it on the kitchen table. We looked in amazement for we had never seen, handled or had close contact with weapons. I picked up the snub nose Saturday night special, it was black pretty and heavy. Just holding it gave one a sense of invincibility and power. Iron a fucking snake, he exclaimed. I think he trying to set me up, and I aint going out like no chump, he grabbed both guns off the table and held them across his chest. Flipping the kitchen chair around 360 degrees he sat down and staring at us intently. Let me ask you all a question, do you like money? He pushed the chair forward leaning in closer. I'm tired of fucking with these Rastas, I'm about to get this paper for self. Peering around the room he gaged the strength of his words by the expressions reflected on our faces. Looking exasperated Cleveland sighed, Iron trying to play me, I made him shine, now he is trying cut my hours and give some dread clown my spot! I'm going to rob him for all the weed and the crack, watch me. He was dead serious, he motioned widely with his hands as though making a silent oath.

Sitting down slowly Cleveland stroked the hairs on his chin while silently contemplating his next move. The silence was thick as day old grits, we all pondered how we would fit in this grand scheme Cleveland was about to hatch. I got it! Cleveland rose to his feet abruptly breaking the silence like a glass bottle against a brick wall. This is what we are going to do, he turned his attention to my cousin Keith. Keith was a bugged-out motherfucker that never backed down from a dare. On one occasion he ran through Tilden projects butt ass naked in the dead of winter on a dare; on another occasion he strolled down rockaway avenue in drag with a dress, wig, lipstick, make up and shoes on, all on a dare; so, if anything, he was the nigga to take any and all kinds of risk regardless of circumstance.

We going to open our own dope spot, we going to pump weed, crack and coke, and get paid, but I need yall to help me rob the spot. We all shook our heads in unison but in our hearts most of us didn't agree. Keith, Cleveland beckoned with his eyes, I need you to get with Iron right hand man Dexter so he can put you on, don't tell him you know me, just act like you need work in shit so he can start you off as a look out.

Keith didn't give a fuck he was down for whatever. Looking towards me and DJ Cleveland continued: once they put Keith on, I can steal all the drugs, the weed and the money, break through the back wall of the building once my shift is over; because this nigga iron keep his workers locked inside the spot with a chain on the door". Once I break out Keith you can help me move the stash, and we can meet up with you and DJ at an undisclosed location and divide the cash; I'm telling you this shit is foolproof, trust me.

The plan was underway, by next weekend Keith did as he was instructed, he loitered around irons spot asking for work because he was trying to get on. As instructed, he finally met up with Dexter and ran the gift of gab on him- Keith was good like that, he had friends everywhere because he was a real charmer. Like clockwork Keith got put on as a lookout by the end of the week.

Me and DJ were instructed to meet Cleveland on Powell street on bikes and stash a portion of the drug loot into our knap sacks and meet him in Bushwick at a drug spot he was setting up. But somehow plans never seem to work out as intended when greed and impatience take precedence strategic planning.

Three weeks, two days and thirty-five minutes down to the letter we received the phone call; the shit was about to hit the fan. My intuition must have been peaked; I couldn't explain it, the phone had a different t ring to it, somehow, I knew it would be Cleveland telling us operation "get cream" was about to commence.

Surprisingly I was wrong, it wasn't Cleveland it was Keith calling to tell us this nigga Cleveland done robbed the fucking spot two hours ago. He was supposed to call us and let us know when shit was about to jump off so we could meet up at the appointed destination, however, greed got the best of the nigga, he chose to take the whole stash for self.

Did he call yall? Keith voice quivered with anxiety. Cuz, I have to go… pausing mid-sentence, the tone in his voice was unmistakable it was the sound of fear. The pit of my stomach tightened; shit didn't sound right. Just then the silence was abruptly shattered by a deafening scream of terror, it was Keith begging for mercy. The sounds of breaking glass and the roar of an impending struggle were all that could be heard blaring through the receiver. At that moment the receiver went dead. I knew something had gone terribly wrong. Dialing frantically, I began to feel numb, tears, streamed out my eyes, nose and mouth as I broke down sobbing uncontrollably. I feared the worst, either Keith was dead or worst he was about to die. But one thing was certain Keith was in grave danger, his cover had been blown.

After discovering his spot had been robbed Iron began a viscous shake down of all his workers. Iron even provided snitches and crack heads with two for one bonus specials on crack or weed if they could provide information regarding Cleveland's whereabouts. Within two hours some snitch ass nigga dropped dime, and the finger had been pointed at Keith. Motherfuckers were saying that Keith was Cleveland's right hand man and they planned to rob iron and usurp his lucrative drug empire.

Cleveland's actions not only endangered himself, he endangered the whole crew. We didn't know whether Keith was dead or alive this was only the beginning of a fucked-up situation, and we got ourselves into this shit-all for the love of money. Unfortunately, the reality was more terrible that we could have ever expected.

Captured and held in a cold dark filthy room illuminated by three black candles Keith was being interrogated-ghetto style-by iron and his henchmen. Hand cuffed, Keith was hogged tied bound and blind folded butt naked to a radiator and remained immobilized until iron entered the room. Keith where is my money, where is my drugs and where the hell is Cleveland! Furious, iron rushed across the room and viciously yanked Keith's head back hog spitting in his face. Where is my drugs Yankee boy; spittle's of saliva sprinkled all over Keith's face. Exhausted, Keith managed to mount a barely audible response. Before he could speak Iron slammed his face against the radiator busting his face open like a potato. A viscous gash opened

145

over the bridge of Keith's nose and both his lips were split wide open. Blood flowed freely spilling over the radiator in rivulets changing its color from a bright metallic silver to a dark tomato red. The force of the impact partially knocked Keith unconscious. Dazed, stunned and incoherent his bladder loosened, urine freely ran down his leg staining the rotted wood planked floor. Awakened by a splash of ammonia to his face, Keith struggled in vain in a futile attempt to free himself from his tormentors. In terror at the plight of what could be his impending death Keith adrenaline began to flow. It was either 'fight or flight'; he would not die this way-beaten, battered and naked, lying in his own waste. If it was his day to die, he would do so on his own terms-like a man.

Mustering all the strength from the core of his being, Keith began screaming like an enraged animal yanking and pulling at his cuffs and bonds. Surprised by Keith's energetic zeal to free himself, Iron and his workers were momentarily taken aback by his response. Ya trying to flee yankee boy, screamed Iron whipping out a mac-10 machine gun. Me got something for you boy. Motioning with his hand, six crack heads entered the room. Two were armed with shovels, the rest remained unarmed. Attacking on command, these crack head attacked like trained dogs. Miraculously, Keith had been able to free both feet and one of his hands during his berserk tirade and cowered in a semi-fetal position to ward off their blows. The next hour and a half he was kicked, scratched, bitten and beaten about his head and body with shovels, fist, hand, feet and teeth. Any one of lesser character would have perished, but Keith's will to persist made him stronger than a motherfucker.

As quickly as the barrage began it ended. It was a though they were under a hypnotic spell. The feigns quickly departed the room. Keith began to realize that they didn't want to kill him...not yet that is. He was being tortured. Iron was going to make an example of him. For if he and Cleveland could rob irons spot and there were no repercussions, irons infamous reputation would be tarnished. His rivals would begin to challenge his control of the New Lots avenue drug trade and his dominance would be threatened. Keith's mind raced uncontrollably; his body ached from what felt like a million open wounds. He was battered bloody and bruised, however he had an idea that if executed properly would work in his favor. Covered from head to toe in blood he began to rub his cuffed hand on the open bloody gash on his leg inflicted by one of his tormentors with the blunted edge of shovel. Blood flowed freely down the iron cuffs lubricating the space between Keith's manacles and the torn flesh of his wrist. Like an animal in a trap, he would not wait for his tormentor to return and put him to death; he would rather chew off his right hand and free himself before allowing that to happen. His hand was now thoroughly saturated with his blood, Keith placed both feet firmly against the rusted radiator and began pushing with every ounce of his strength to free his hand from his shackles. His hand throbbing in pain, Keith continued to pull against his manacles. He felt as though his arms had reached their breaking point, the cords in his contorted limbs felt as though they would snap. Keith's body convulsed with tension as sweat flowed freely down the nape of his back into the crack of his ass. Slowly his hand began slipping through the cuff. The cold dank blood-stained iron racked his flesh of his wrist to the white meat, but his instinct to survive was the overriding factor that nullified the pain and fear he now experienced. Now focused, he began contemplating how he would escape once freed from his bonds. The cuffs-which had now reached the midpoints of Keith's hand strangled every nerve fiber in his palm. Gnawing on his tongue, Keith squinted his eyes and moaned in pain. Tears streamed down his eyes-but his hands were almost free. The pain was excruciating; his hands were now numb and were pealed like bananas, yet he continued to pull. With his blood now constricted Keith circulation was cut off in his hand. He no longer felt pain; this was a blessing in disguise.

Sensing the urgency which now confronted him, with the last ounce of his strength Keith violently jerked at his bond with such force that not only did his hand pop loose from its bond, the radiator ripped from its foundation throwing him back suddenly. Keith fell like a sack of bricks; his naked bruised body crashed to the dank filthy hard wood floor with such force he feared he would fall right through. Like a panther, within milliseconds he bounded to his feet. What seemed like an eternity had transpired in all over three minutes. Keith's eyes scoured the room searching meticulously for a route by which to make his escape. His eyes laid transfixed to the padlocked exit that had now been adorned with a thick heavy chain. Now on his feet, Keith crept through the dark expanse of the room feeling along the walls for hollow pockets. Knowing all that lied between freedom or death was perhaps a few feet of sheet rock and wood. Keith resigned himself to the idea that his only means of escape would be to somehow tunnel through the back of the wall.

Continuing to search for a means of escape, Keith became seemingly more frantic as he heard iron and his posse quickly advancing on his position. Perhaps he had been heard... perhaps they wanted him to escape in the hopes they would target him with a rifle-shooting him in his back as he fled. One thing was certain, he would not be leaving the way that he came. Grabbing the radiator, Keith mustered all his remaining strength and dead lifted the radiator above his head.

Rushing toward the wall, Keith drove the radiator into the high end of the old rotted dilapidated wall with such force that he and the radiator slammed through the sheet rock almost effortlessly. Paint chips dust and molded wood showered the floor; the chalky mildew filled the air covering Keith's face hair and body. Keith began digging through the wall with his bare hands. He tore at the remaining pieces of plywood and sheet rock in the wall clearing a three- and one-half inch hole large enough to scramble through. At that moment Keith heard the rustling of keys. Keith's breath shortened; his heart began to race uncontrollably, adrenaline raced through every artery in his body. The bolt locked door was being opened. There was no time to climb through the small opening in the wall and safety access the outside perimeter. Keith knew he had to get the fuck out of the room immediately or he'd be dead. Backing up quickly, Keith gave himself running room. At that moment he burst forth exploding into a full gallop like an Olympic sprinter. Battered-bruised and naked as the day he was born-he ran. With every muscle, every fiber in his being-he ran. Today was not his day to die he reasoned; he would die an old man surrounded by a bunch of bitches and their nappy headed children. They would not find his cold maggot infested bullet riddled body in the back of some abandoned fucking building, he pondered.

Running headlong toward the small gaping hole in the wall, Keith clenched his teeth and tightened every muscle in his body bracing himself as he prepared to crash though the wall. Just as he neared the wall, the chain on the lock bolted door gave way falling to the floor. Iron and his Hench men abruptly entered the room carrying machetes, axes, and handguns. Covering his face and the top of his head with both forearms, Keith lunged with all his might headfirst crashing though the enclosure. His naked flesh now covered in protruding splinters; Keith fell hard to the ground of the brick strewn rubble filled lot. With pain now secondary, Keith quickly rose to his feet and began running barefoot across glass, brick, garbage and rocks oblivious to the damage inflicted on the soles of his feet.

Brandishing two 45's, iron rushed toward the gaping hole at the back of the room, crouched to one knee and began firing; shells spat from the chambers of both weapons littering the floor. Bullets whizzed past Keith head as he ran in a zig-zag pattern to avoid being hit by irons hollow tip shells. Nearing the edge of the garbage strewed lot Keith vaulted toward the barbed wire fence. Kicking off the gate Keith leaped frogged several feet into the air tearing the flesh from his left buttock, and rib, as the razor wire found its mark. Keith fell hard to the pavement and was stunned momentarily. Rattled, he rose to his feet and ran naked into oncoming traffic causing cars to screech to a grinding halt.

Neither iron nor his team followed their prey for fear of being identified by witnesses. On lookers gawked in terror as Keith nakedly stumbled through the streets in a semi-conscious state; Keith continued to run several more blocks without looking back. Fear had a way of moving people in mysterious ways; some became immobilized, while others became supermen, Keith represented the latter. The overriding emotion fueling Keith's desperate attempts at escape was not fear-not on the contrary-it was anger. Keith pondered how Cleveland in his stupidity could betray his trust. Pondering his situation, his anger intensified. He could be dead by now had it not been for his herculean efforts to evade his captors. As he continued running Keith was now furious, he now earnestly sought to track Cleveland down. Martial artist or not, when he caught up with Cleveland his intention was to whip that niggas ass.

As Keith dragged his battered bloody carcass through the streets, his mind raced widely. His eyes darted to and for searching for a means of escape. A blood slick trail lined the streets leaving tale-tale signs of his passing. Trudging forward, blood continued to pour into his eyes, every muscle burned, and each step became labored as he fought to maintain consciousness. Adrenaline pulsed through his veins as his mind struggled to recall addresses, names and faces of friends he had in the area.

In a moment of clarity, he recalled the one person he knew he could vaguely count upon- Charles. Charles was an old Vietnam veteran who used to tell war stories and school me about all that counterintelligence and CIA stuff. After returning home from Vietnam, he brought a house on Hinsdale avenue in east New York and hooked back with

Vicky- Cleveland Aunt -who he was previously engaged to prior to leaving for Vietnam in 1971. However, once he found out she had a baby by some bum mother fucker-who dumped her, all that lovey dove shit changed. He now regarded Vicky as only a dumb ass piece of pussy, he treated her like a stepchild; a house servant. When Charles came from Nam, he was doing quite well for himself, on the other hand, Vicky was a single mother on welfare, she naturally latched on to Charles as he was her first love. Charles was bitter and vindictive, he would make Vicky pay for her betrayal, by treating her like a prostitute. He made her work around his home cleaning the floors cooking, and giving him pussy, only to throw her ten to fifteen dollar-back in those days a pretty good sum-per month for her services; he never promised to marry her again.

Staggering towards Hinsdale Street, Keith dared not look back for fear his captors might still be trailing closely behind. His destination was not far off; he had only two more blocks to transverse, however in his present condition two blocks may well have been ten miles. Keith continued to move forward oblivious to the mass of honking horns, stalled traffic and a crowd of onlookers; some indifferent others jubilant waiting in anticipation for a fight; shoot out; or stabbing. They were those who had become desensitized to the violence and looked forward to the dead bodies and blood shed associated with the drug game. Developing tunnel vision, the only thing Keith saw before him was his destination. The world became a silent mass of color and movement as Keith's peripheral vision became blurred; Charles house was the light at the end of the tunnel. It was as though he was in a dream, although he moved as fast as he could, the world revolved in slow motion-the walls of time cascaded into waterfalls of warm molasses. Was this what men experienced moments before death, when they stared down the barrel of a shot gun or a 44 magnum, or as they laid disemboweled on some foreign battlefield riddle from asshole to torso with bullets and shrapnel? The pain was gone, Keith no longer felt his body, he moved forward as though he were disembodied compelled by a spiritual force. As he neared the entrance way of Charles home, he saw a hand; it was his own. Reaching forward as he neared the doorknob, the door swung opened it was Charles. Keith floated into the vestibule and all went black as he lapped into the deep sleep of unconsciousness. Keith laid in a semi coma for the next three days. He was nursed back to health by Charles with a variety of soups hot and cold compress and some good old fashion bed side manner.

CHAPTER 16   DRUG DEALING

Cleveland got over like a fat rat he robbed Iron's most profitable drug den stealing 20 ounces of weed, over a dozen eight balls of crack rock, and thirteen hundred dollars in cash- total street value over 29 thousand dollars' worth of shit to muscle to build his new hustle. It took Keith two months to recover from his injuries after Iron and his crew damn near killed him. Naturally Keith was mad like a mother fucker and didn't want to have shit to do with Cleveland, however Cleveland needed someone he could trust, he couldn't fuck with no crack head motherfucker's and have them watching over his drug spot, that would have been a dumb ass move. Cleveland needed Keith, he needed all of us, and so he called Keith and met up with him in Unity Plaza Park on Williams between Blake and Dumont Avenue. Walking with a limp, Keith entered the Blake avenue side of the park and silently approached Cleveland, every muscle in his body tensed with seething anger. Cleveland smiled and walked towards Keith with his hands outstretched as though Keith were his long-lost lover. What's good cousin, Cleveland replied feigning sincerity as though he honestly gave a damn. I heard what happened, that was kind of fucked up, but I tried to call you, but I had to break out, the time was just right Kid. Cleveland saw the seething hatred in Keith's eyes. He knew he had to do something to de-escalate the situation because he needed allies, he already had a shit load of enemies and didn't need any addition ones.

Cleveland was a master at reading body language; it was one of the many talents that kept him alive and ahead of the viscous drug game. He already anticipated Keith would swing on him and was already two steps ahead of him. "I could have been dead motherfucker", Keith replied as he approached Cleveland with his hand clenched in a fist. Erupting like a dead volcano Keith exploded forth at lightning speed charging at Cleveland. Keith threw a jab and a left hook with knock out power in viscous attempt to break Cleveland mother fucking jaw. Cleveland dipped to the right and threw a left-hand fan block parrying Keith's jab with ease; however, the hook caught Cleveland on his floating ribs. Knocking the air directly out of his lungs, Cleveland collapsed to the pavement. The toughest mother fucker couldn't take that blow and still be standing. Cleveland was panting for air crouched in a fetal position as Keith stood over Cleveland- eyes aflame- in a fighting stance. Rolling over Cleveland smiled, you got that cousin, that was a good fucking punch. But I'm not hear for that.

Cleveland rose to one knee. I'm here to make you a proposal. Cleveland reached into his pocket and pulled out ten thousand dollars in cold hard cash, throwing it to the pavement. I can't change what happened in the past but perhaps I can make up for it". Cleveland reached to the pavement picking up the heavy wad of cash wrapped in thick rubber bands and placed it into Keith's hand. You paid your dues, you a mother fucking trooper." "Niggers know your name, now it's time to claim your fame". "You the only mother fucker who ever fronted on iron and lived to tell about it." "Word on the street is that you fought off twenty mother fuckers with your bare hands; I'm proud of you nigger; that aint no small feat. Keith ate Cleveland's bullshit like a kid in a candy store. Obsessed with gaining some semblance of power, Keith sought any means to repair his deflated ego, running the bullshit on how he was now a ghetto celebrity was a sure fire means re-gaining Keith's confidence. Looking at the money in his hand Keith quickly held it next to his ear flicking the cash with his thumb like a deck of playing cards. His eyes widened as he realized there were only hundred-dollar bills in his stash. Smiling, Keith placed the money in his side pocket and reached forth his hand grasping Cleveland wrist pulling him up to a standing position. Now eye to eye, Cleveland embraced Keith patting him on his back. "Keith this money is only the tip of the iceberg me and you have a chance to get large. Fuck iron I got twenty ounces of weed a dozen eight balls of crack and twenty thousand dollars in my pocket for startup cost. We are going to do this shit for ourselves. As Cleveland spoke, he eyed Keith closely looking for signs of approval. With ten gees in his pocket Keith now felt like the man. "Fuck it", Keith exclaimed. "I'm down". It was better than being a punk ass look out for some coconut, he pondered.

Cleveland and Keith found a prime location for the drug spot they were going to front on Chauncey Street in Bushwick. The spot was a building recently abandoned for renovation and was perfect for a startup. The spot was in prime territory near Broadway partially under the elevated J train station. At night this part of town was home to the "walking dead"- crack heads, dope fiends, and homeless motherfuckers. People out there were below the bottom of barrel they would think a homeless shelter was the Marriott hotel.

156

Me and DJ knew Keith would fall right back into the game once he got some 'scratch' in his pocket. All that bullshit he was talking about not fucking with Cleveland and getting out of the game was exactly what it was-bullshit! Right after he caught up with Cleveland those niggas went on a shopping spree like a motherfucker. In order to be recognized as the proverbial drug-dealer you had to look and dress the part. Back in the crack cocaine era, drug dealers represented a class of hustler who exuded style finesses in addition to an allure of danger. In order to become a ghetto superstar, you had to have flash with your cash; you had to shine while you were on your grind. Or bitches would think you were a nickel and dime half stepping scrub; a look out or a drug carrier, that shit was for little niggers, working for sneaker and weed money, shit like that wasn't good for a nigga's reputation.

Keith and Cleveland began a lavish shopping spree to re-up on all the fly shit. They ran through Pitkin Avenue, Downtown Brooklyn's Albee Square Mall, Delancey Street, Dapper Dans in Harlem, Fordham Road in the Bronx, and Jamaica Avenue shopping centers. Cleveland copped the suede and leather Bailey's all flavors, Wallaby Clarks, Playboys, gators and Stacy Adams. Keith copped the fly 40-inch Gucci Link with the Mother Mary plate sized medallion, diamond crusted gold fronts, and satin and silk shirts of all flavors. Never one to be outdone, Cleveland upped the ante and copped a brand-new mint silver nickel plated Volvo coup with cream color leather interior. The whip was fitted with mobile phone, hi-fi stereo system, with hidden gun rack and liquor bar. Rolling through with the fly pussy mobile, Keith and Cleveland glided down Livonia

Avenue fronting hard. Cleveland had the coup freshly glazed with jet black limo tints. Heads turned as they slid down the avenue bumping Eric B. for President. Heads recognized true players and gave niggers the nod signifying their approval of their new-found status. Seated in the whip on a 45-degree incline Cleveland responded to their non-verbal overtures by lowering the automatic windows half-way throwing his subjects the peace sign; his fingers and wrist crusted with Jewels and diadems like an African King.

Keith and Cleveland rolled into the parking lot. All eyes were on them, the front of the building usually a hub of all types of activity came to a screeching halt. Gangster chicks fly bitches and B-girls hovered around the freshly dipped vehicle like bees attracted to honey, or more so like flies attracted to shit. Shari, a bow-legged gold tooth ho who could suck a mean dick and had a reputation for getting the hardest motherfuckers strung the fuck out approached the driver's side of the vehicle and wiggled her petit frame halfway into the window.

Like a serpent Shari gently slid her hand down the nape of Cleveland's neck and whispered in his ear. "Daddy I see you balling hard, how about you put that ball in my hoop". Cleveland Knew Shari's reputation and wasn't trying to fuck with her at all, he had other shit on his mind. He knew she was skilled at fucking; she got his dick hard just talking in his ear. Pulling out a wad of cash from a money clip he had tucked in his waistline, Cleveland coldly stared at Shari and brushed her off replying, "my money is my bitch", waving the knot of cash before her eyes. "This bitch is always by my side and gives me anything I want, and don't ask for shit in return, only to be held. In one motion Shari rolled her eyes and neck, sucked her teeth, flicked her right hand and placed her left on protruding hips, and glared at him sarcastically. Nigga you scared, probably got a little ass dick anyway, you know if I gave you a piece of this pussy trust me, you'll be strung. Shari turned walking away exposing her magnificent ass. Viewing this spectacle from the fifth story window, DJ rushed excitedly into the living room. Ale you have to see this, he bellowed. Rushing toward the window I drew up the windowpane and called down to Cleveland below. Cleveland looked up as he exited the Volvo and Keith followed closely behind entering the building. In haste I quickly dressed, I was ready to roll out in the pussy mobile; for a day I wanted to know what it felt like to be a ghetto superstar. Rushing to the living room I moved toward the door quickly looking through the peek hole awaiting the arrival of my cousins like a virgin on a first date. "Here they come", me and DJ quickly threw on our coats and stepped into our sneakers. The iron project door vibrated from the incessant knocking signaling their arrival. Like an excited bitch on prom night I swung open the door and snatched Cleveland up in a steely embrace giving him a soul pound. Looking him up and down he was draped from head to toe in red wallabies, red leather pants, red silk shirts, and red furry Kangol fedora. What's up, Cleveland replied as he swaggered past DJ and me flopping on the couch. We stood in awe and fascination at our cuz who overnight appeared to transform from rags to riches.

Rising to his feet like an elder statesman Cleveland began his preamble to win our hearts and minds. I was already sold after viewing how the hood reacted. I wanted in; however, I didn't want to appear too anxious. I would let

159

him run down the plan just to see where his head was. Cleveland stood on his feet in quiet contemplation; he stared at each of us gauging our level of attention. Rubbing his chin, he paced the floor slowly looking forward as if his perception were focused on the future.

Abruptly the silence was broken as he began to speak. Popping the collar of his red silk shirt Cleveland exclaimed, seize the day! Cleveland paced back and forth with silent power as he weighed his words carefully as he contemplated his words.

Seize the day! I'm tired of seeing the Arabs, Puerto Ricans, and Dominicans with their own businesses. I'm tired of seeing the Rastas with their drug spots and were always on the outside looking in. Were always nickel and diming we have to be about our business! The Drug trade is about supply and demand. Nobody ever gave me shit! Aint no white man going to give me a business loan; you either, Cleveland pointed at us; his index finger was heavy and sparked with gold diamonds and other rare baubles. Gathering his thoughts Cleveland continued his oratory, "Nigga how you think you going to get rich, how you think you going to get power… Huh! "Power is never given it is seized". "This is power"!! Cleveland pulled three stacks of hundreds, his 45 magnum and a pound of weed and slammed it on the table. "You seize the supply my nigga and you can make the motherfucking demands". None of us dared speak; Cleveland held the floor, as we lay entranced upon his words. You think you getting rich by packing bags at the supermarket, by being a messenger or a security guard…Huh. A fucking worker will always remain at the bottom, the Kennedy's, the Rockefellers, Rothschild's, and the Bushes were all a bunch of thieves, robber barons, drug dealers, and bootleggers. But the difference between them and us is they seized the day. These motherfuckers have never done and honest days' work in their whole lives. They never worked a nine to five, they seized the supply, made the demands and got mother fuckers to work for them. These shysters made millions, flipped the game and became legit with bootleg liquor, drug and blood money. They put their kids through Harvard, Yale and Oxford, from criminals they became members of Americas ruling class, that's what I'm trying to, I'm trying to leave a dynasty. No minimum wage job is going to get me what I need. As I listened to Cleveland, my mind was mired in chaos, my whole moral compass was in danger of being shattered. His words seared my mind like a branding iron. I thought back to how my mother and aunty struggled from check to check, how they were swamped with bills, how they couldn't make ends meet, how on various occasions our refrigerator lay empty-the only thing remaining in its hollowed-out belly was bacon-soda and a pitcher of water. I recalled how me, and DJ had to go to free lunch, our mothers had to stand on food lines to get free cheese, butter, bread, powdered milk, and no-frills cereals; she did all this shit and she had a job. Albeit she was one of the working-class poor and made only enough to barely survive. To add insult to injury, the system wouldn't even give her a break by providing food stamp assistance because they said she made to much money.

In contrast the graveyards and the prisons were filled with Black men with grandiose dreams of becoming kingpins of lucrative drug empires. The streets bore testimony of stolen and crushed dreams, broken men, the drug addicted, and those who wasted away lost in forgotten dreams of yesterday. Now voiceless, in their alcohol and drug induced haze they spoke of times past in nostalgic tones full of pain and remembering. Their guttural words spoke dark tales of sorrow and regret, of goals not accomplished of dreams not fulfilled. The night air was full solemn testimonies and words full of sorrow... I could have... should have... would have, was their mantra that vibrated off the brick solid walls in the bowels of the ghetto. In this nightmarish world of poverty, the drug game afforded superficial dreams, temporary riches, and a life full of suffering and pain.

I remember the lesson my mother taught me all too well. She showed me the results of players who eventually got played, ballers who fouled out of the game, and stickup kids who eventually reaped what they sowed; the prisons; the graveyards; those in wheelchairs and those on death row illustrated this fact all too well. As I listened to Cleveland inspirational tirade, I pondered whether the ends justified the means. Was I willing to risk everything; my life, my freedom and my sanity all for the temporary bliss of attaining the ghetto's version of the 'American Dream-with its money, clothes and & hoes? These were the traps my mother had so vigorously warned me of. What would make Cleveland's plan so fool proof? Others had come down this path before; the Nicky Barnes, Frank Lucas, Bumpy Johnson, & Alpo's of the world all lost their freedom due to betrayal by members of their own team. These were the best whoever did it, and even they eventually failed, betrayed by their own partners, girlfriends & snitches. It was always for the same old things jealously, greed, and power, these were the evils that affected the hearts and minds of men. This was a disease and those contaminated passed their malady to others. In the end the love of money ruled all, and it was this desire for crass materialism that led men to this insatiable need for power. However, I was only a man, a young man, frail and full of faults. I was attracted by the material love of riches, power, fame and bitches. My desire ruled over my logic. My adolescent feelings of invincibility- naïve as they were- convinced me that I only had one life to live, and I wanted mines now…not tomorrow, because tomorrow is promised no man. I pondered, I'd rather die a young man having tasted the fruits of life, than an old working-class sucker who was disciplined, saved money and suddenly dropped dead; all his riches going to some bitch and undeserving children.

This must have been the temptation Christ felt as he as was taken to the heights and shown the world in all its glory by Satan who promised all would be his if only, he bowed and gave his soul. Would I bow, I pondered? Would I give my allegiance to lust, greed & power all for the need to appease my materialistic desires? This was the temptation the forbidden fruit that God forbade man from eating. I stood at the crossroads. I understood right from wrong and good from evil, was I willing to lose my soul for a few shekels of gold, like Judas who sold out the Christ for that of a few coins. Would I betray my morals and values to be the man for a minute, or work hard, stay the straight and narrow path, hopefully reaching that pie in the sky reward promised by the saints? My mind was made, I was a risk taker and not a faker. I would strive to be a baller and a shot caller…fuck it! The ends justified the means and if I could find a shortcut to the road to the riches then why would I go through hell and high water to get there.

Operations began in earnest. Cleveland copped a bulk of materials such as bacon soda, ammonia, measuring scales, hot plates, bowls, measuring cups, salt and other drug paraphernalia, shit it looked like a nigga was opening a bakery. This was the wares of a ghetto chief, a motherfucker who plied his trade in the dope game. Cleveland was trying to beat the middleman; if he cooked his own product, he would save 50% in startup cost. Me, DJ and Keith thought the nigga had crack rock; this nigga had pure uncut coke. He was sitting on Seventy-five thousand dollars; all we had to do was convert that pure powder white into street product...crack. It wasn't the 22 thousand dollars we originally thought Cleveland stuck Iron for. "Never let your right hand know what your left had is doing", Cleveland said as he boiled buckets of water in preparation to cook the product. "You think I would risk my ass for some bullshit ass 22 thousand dollars nigga". Cleveland reached into his pocket and pulled out a mint tossing it on the table. "I used to make 15 long every two weeks; yawl should know me better than that".

Cleveland cooked and prepared product for two hours, we all sat in the dilapidated vacant apartment house on Chauncey Street. We powered up the lights on the first floor in the back room of the building with makeshift lamps we ran from the streetlights outside. Keith ran to the store and copped some Kentucky Fried Chicken and three forty ounces. We ate, drank and got fucked up. Cleveland pulled a Dutch and began rolling some weed. As I sucked the chicken grease off my fingers and lapped up some mash potatoes, I watched Cleveland crack the Dutch, his fingers worked their magic cutting the cigar down the middle. His thumbs worked adroitly spilling the tobacco residue into the ceramic ashtrays. Cleveland then began performing fellatio on the Dutch paper. His tongue explored the outer edges of the cigar paper and angled down the middle gently licking vertically; his saliva stroked smooth the paper which opened and relaxed in preparation for the herbal sperm which would be laid at its center. I wasn't into running the train or playing sloppy seconds but in this case, I was willing to puff, puff and pass. The ganja was light green and smelled fresh like clean cut grass dripping with dew in the morning. I had never smoked weed - I tried to in the past, but the shit I smoked was that dirt weed…that shit that had more seeds than weed.

Cleveland fingers continued working mechanistically rolling the saliva shellacked cigar leaf in a semi-circle counterclockwise motion until the Dutch was hermetically sealed. It was a masterpiece. Cleveland held up the Dutch eyeing his creation like a proud father. We sat on the makeshift black leather couch and cracked our second forty-ounce and began pouring ghetto libations in homage to the brothers no longer here. With his right thumb Cleveland flicked the lighter sparking the torch; its flame gently caressed the base of the Dutch. Cleveland waived the lighter back and forth ensuring the leaf was devoid of moisture. Gripping the forty I held the bottle close to my chest like a long-lost lover. I wanted to escape from reality. I wanted to forget the fear, anxiety and internal turmoil permeating my mind. No longer did I want to hear that inner voice- call it God or Angel, I wanted to live by my own rules. I wanted to be the law unto myself; I would worry about the consequences of my actions later, but for now I wanted to get fucked up. With authority I raised the forty taking it straight to the head downing damn near eight ounces of the ghetto elixir in one sitting. Sluggishly I passed the forty to the left aggressively pushing it into the hands of my man DJ. Take it to the head motherfucker, I bellowed. Keith quickly turned looked at me and exploded in uproarious laughter. Slapping his knees, he held his hand on his ribs struggling to catch his breath. Cleveland this nigga aint ready, he only took a sip of the forty and he talking shit. Nigga I'm down for whatever; I pounded my chest three times displaying a foolish juvenile bravado. Eying me suspiciously, Cleveland passed the blunt into my hand. Cuz, you sure you could fuck with this, because I don't want you bugging out. Nigga I got this, I snatched the blunt readily and took it to my dome to prove my manhood. I pulled hard and deeply in a flagrant attempt to capture the very essence of the herb smoke. As I inhaled, the pungent vapors filled my lungs and began its course through my blood stream along to my brain quickly inducing it magic. As the haze slowly oozed out my mouth and nasal cavity, I sat back, arched my head skyward blowing donut shaped billows of weed smoke towards the heavens. Now relaxed, my eyes whittled down to mere slits and were the color of Christ blood. All my fears, inhibitions and worries were now gone. The world slowed to a crawl, yet I was experiencing a profound sense of mental clarity…was I high? Was this the feeling ever nigga sought daily like a long-lost piece of pussy. I now began to understand the reasons mother fuckers had to cop that five-dollar bitch by hook or crook, rain sleet, sun or snow; the high was good!!!

The herbal elixir orbited freely amongst us from mouth to hand, from hand to mouth. We conversed openly discussing our plans to blow up in the drug game. We were each given our task by Cleveland. He explained that we were a team, each of us were a part of a larger body, each of us had a role to play. As the head it was his job to plan formulate and strategize power movements. As the feet of the operation my role; as Cleveland explained, was to steer the marks to our spot, stand as look-out against rival crews and police and screen all potential customers.

Keith would be the arms, he would be responsible for carrying weight, in laymen's terms he would be moving the product-the weed; the crack; the dope from the supplier to the spot. For the moment we didn't have a connect but all the shit we had in our stash would be able to hold us down for two months or more. The cash generated from our sales would be more than enough to buy more kilos when it was time to re-up. DJ would be the torso; the body of the operation. His job would be storage and distribution. Once the shipment was received, he would store, supply, cook, bag and prepare the package for distribution. As the torso also houses the heart, the ribs and the chest; DJ's position lay at the crux of the operation. He was responsible for housing and storing weapons to fortify the spot from invaders.

The weed must have been good. We were brainstorming on a higher level than we ever imagined. Cleveland continued to explain that every part of the body was important; each held and supported the interest of the other. The hands carried the supply much so like it was food for the body of the operation. Once the raw supply was ingested into the body or the torso it would be broken down and digested into the belly and transformed into product. Product would then be distributed and expelled, like shit back into the streets for consumption by feigns who hovered like flies waiting to feed. "This shit is like clockwork", Cleveland explained. "The more we eat the stronger our team becomes, and if we are eating lovely, mother fuckers in these streets going to starve, and trust my nigga I'm a greedy mother fucker, feel me"! And feel him we did, we all laughed in unison slapping hands and giving each other "soul pounds". From that day on like Voltron we transformed into one body-our name was The Get Money Crew.

The streets were hungry, and word traveled fast. The fiends like zombies could smell a new crack spot, they came in droves. The money came fast, and business was good.... too good. It was only half a week later and already we accumulated sixteen thousand dollars. I was anxious as fuck to get fresh; I didn't even get paid but already had plans to spend all my money on sneakers, jewelry, clothes and ho's. As I reflect, boy was I a dumb motherfucker. I couldn't wait to get my loot so I could break change for a fifty or one-hundred-dollar bill, get nothing but singles, roll it into a thick knot of cash and place three to four hundred crispy dollar bills on top. I wanted to flash my stash of cash to drive the ladies crazy. However, little did I know our dreams would soon become a nightmare as we were eating too good and sleeping too hard while our enemies starved and watched us with envious eyes.

We underestimated Irons resourcefulness. He was well known, connected and dangerous. He was a general in the drug game. He was a front man at the beginning of a drug pipeline that extended from New York to Columbia. He got his shit directly from Columbian foot soldiers-the pure uncut raw. He was the main distributor in the New York area; he supplied crews in all five boroughs. All the hustlers bought directly from him; he fed the streets. He was respected, loved and most of all he was feared. Others who had been foolishly brazen enough to rob his spots before, their dismembered bodies had been found in garbage bags; a thanksgiving feast for wild dogs. Iron had enough coke to take a hit and not even ruffle his pockets; but he could not let any level of disrespect go unchallenged, he had a reputation to uphold. He could not let a group of unknown upstarts steal from his table; any motherfucker who violated had to be dealt with or made an example of. Our time was numbered; we had been marked for death. A price had been put on our heads, but this time it was personal, Iron wanted to pull the trigger himself. The word was out, anyone offering information regarding Cleveland whereabouts would be granted a thousand dollars; but he wanted us alive so he could reward himself by completing the dirty deed. Iron had eyes, ears, hands, feet and arms in the streets. He had motherfuckers who were bonafide killers, willing to die for him and ask for seconds. He was part of a well-connected underworld network who if you were not a member you were an enemy and a threat. Had I known; I would have never vowed to take part in a suicide mission. I was seduced by the lure of fast money and wasn't thinking straight. I was deceived by outward appearances; I wanted to be a don. I wanted to be like Cleveland and one day open my own drug spot. I wanted to be like Al Pachinko and blow up rising from rags to riches; boy was I a fool!

The day of reckoning came faster than a young boy getting his first piece of pussy. Our customer base began to dry up as word out on the streets were that we were responsible for robbing the most powerful drug lord in the five boroughs. Cleveland shut down our lucrative operation; it had become too dangerous for us to operate. Paranoia had now set in. As we tightened our level of security, every customer that copped weed, coke or crack was treated like a potential enemy; they were patted down and searched for weapons at gun point. A price was on our heads, and we responded accordingly. Any motherfucker; crack head; dope fiend or otherwise could have been a potential assassin; niggas wasn't taking no chances.

Cleveland split up the cut 80/20. He kept the entire stash of weed, coke and crack in addition to twenty-five thousand in cash. Keith took ten thousand in cash and kept two ounces of weed for his troubles. Me and DJ got five-gees. Cleveland was planning to transport his operation down south to Virginia or to the Midwest as those markets were untapped and crews that fucked virgin territory usually got rich.

Greed got the best of us, instead of continuing our operations we decided to go on a massive shopping spree. Niggas had money and lots of it. I wasn't planning on getting no 401-K investing in CD's, IRA's or looking to diversify my stock portfolio; we didn't know anything about that shit. We had money, we were young, and we were going to get fly, get bitches, rock jewels and floss to the fucking wheels fell off. We went shopping hitting up all the hot spots. I bought about ten pair of sneakers. I copped Adidas, Pumas, Sergio Tacchini, Clarks, Playboys, British Walkers, three

170

pairs of Bali's a couple of Lee suits, leather pants, suede fronts, a red rag Kangol and a name ring. The rest of the loot I kept in my pocket. I didn't know the next time I would come across that much change, so I had to maintain my composure even though the money was burning in my pocket.

After our elaborate shopping spree, we came to the hood laden with bags. Everyone went to DJ's house got showered dressed and decided to go to Coney Island. Cleveland hit the car wash; armor oiled the tires and had the Volvo looking fresh. We all got dipped headed out to the "Island" to hang out at Nathans and rap with bitches. It was the perfect summer night; we drank three 40's, smoked two bags of weed and chilled to the wee hours of the morning by the Disco Express. Little did we know that night we were not alone; unbeknownst lurking in the shadows Iron and his team watched and surveyed our movements like lions stalking their prey. Me, DJ, Keith & Cleveland flicked it up with mad shorty's, I caught five numbers just doing a gangster lean by the concession stand. I rocked a blood red leather front, a pair of hard blue Levi denim jeans, a red furry Kangol slicked down with baby oil, white BVD nylon tank top, red fingerless gloves, red Pumas, some Guess spectacles, a 24inch Herring Bone chain and three initial rings on both hands; I was the man to say the least. Cleveland was on that Jamaican shit. He wore an electric blue satin shirt, shark skin pants, light blue Bali's, a rope chain with the Jesus Medallion piece, a four-finger ring on both hands with two diamond pinky rings. He didn't rock a hat; he had the S-curl with a skin fade rocking a mouth full of gold. He held a Heineken at the tip of his fore finger which suavely

171

dangled at his side exposing his gold nugget encrusted watch. DJ was the artistic one of the bunch he had his Levi suit tailored to perfection. His Levi denims had the permanent crease, his jacket was emblazoned with a color filled Disney Towel with Mickey and Mini Mouse adorning his back and elbows. He rocked a bell-shaped rag patterned Kangol, lens less Cazal's a blue and white striped cotton short sleeved shirt; and a baby Gucci link with the initials DJ dangling across his chest adorned in 24 carat gold. He was hip hop fresh and was hugged up with two honeys. Oblivious to the smell of death in the air we partied like rock stars till 4 o'clock in the morning which came quickly. We paid no heed to time on that warm summer night by the boardwalk on the shores of Coney Island. As quickly as it began the party ended on a high note. The sounds of laughter joking, and flirting could be heard a block away. Cleveland & Keith both caught dime pieces; one light skinned freckled face thick almond eye cutie straddled Cleveland waists passionately giving him tongue while his hand freely roamed her thighs. Keith had the other chick hemmed up against a light pole fondling her breast ass and tattooing her neck with hicky's. It was 1987, tity sucking was the rage back then. I was saddled with a caramel complexioned Dominican chick. We did some heavy petting and foreplay for what it was worth, but she had Sergio Valente skintight denims on, the most she would let me do was dry hump through her jeans while we lay in the sand. I had blue balls like a motherfucker; I had semen welling up at the tip of my cock, however at the end of the day it was worth it. On the other hand, DJ was on some romantic fantasy shit, he walked the beach barefooted tonguing his bitch while carrying her in his arms; the waves roaring against his feet. It worked, she jumped on his dick and was sprung; we laughed about it later in the car as we sped down the highway on our way back to Brownsville.

Although Cleveland had bravado and the heart of a lion, we were sleeping. We were drinking Bacardi Dark, Heineken and smoking "L's" all night and bragging about how many numbers we copped. Had we forgot the many lessons the drug game afforded; the countless Dons who got bodied in their prime thinking shit was sweet. Cleveland was slipping; or perhaps he was simply being reckless. Whipping the Volvo, he roared off the Belt Parkway burning rubber as he skidded down the ramp on Pennsylvania Avenue doing ninety miles per hour. We sped towards New Lots Avenue, while two car lengths behind Iron and crew followed closely patiently anticipating the moment to swizz cheese the Volvo, cut Cleveland throat, burn the vehicle and slaughter every one of us leaving no witnesses. Although high, something just didn't feel right. Intuition made my stomach tingle and the hairs on my neck rise all over my body. That little voice; or what I commonly referred to as my consciousness never led me wrong. I would not be distracted by my marijuana and liquor induced haze. I was determined to convince Cleveland to change course and take another route. Cleveland how the fuck you gonna roll through the same area you did dirt in, I said exasperated by his apparent lack of caution. Cleveland eyed me suspiciously shifting uncomfortably in the driver's seat for a moment before suddenly pivoting 180 degrees whipping out a German Luger 45 automatic pistol laying it on the wood paneled arm rest. Don't tell me you scared cuz, that's why I didn't want yall down with this shit. Gritting my teeth, I began perspiring, my adrenaline was flowing. I was angry and at the point of exploding. I was not going to back down. Apparently, Cleveland didn't give a fuck about his life or ours. He was a classic sociopath; Keith was almost murdered because of his actions. I would make it a point to let him know I would not be next. Viciously scowling I raised both my hands parallel to my face pointing them in his direction. Roaring from the gut I cried, "Turn the fucking car down Georgia dumbass we got a price on our heads". Cleveland was taken aback and surprised by my reaction. Although I respected him, he stared straight into my eyes and knew I would not back down. He paused shrugged his shoulders and smirked nodding in silent agreement. All right family If you that shook, I'll take an alternate route to get us the fuck back home.

We took an alternate route turning down Georgia avenue and began driving toward Blake avenue; there we would make the left and travel due west crossing under the elevated train station till we arrived at Van Dyke Projects. However, the journey would not end that simply. As we crossed town, I discovered the source of my intuitive premonitions. Peering towards the rear-view window I observed what appeared to be a black van with tinted windows tailing us; its front lights were barely visible as it had been turned to the lowest setting. At first, I didn't pay it any mind, perhaps I was being paranoid. However, after reaching Blake Avenue and making the left turn as we anticipated, the van continued following us at a minimal distance to appear as though it was traveling at a normal speed. Cleveland noticed too, peering in his rear-view mirror; he began to speed up to put some distance between himself and this unknown assailant. As we neared our destination, I turned looking to spot the vehicle, however like an apparition the van had vanished like a ghost. As we neared the parking lot Cleveland whipped the Volvo making a sharp left around the parking post up the short ramp. As the Volvo slid easily amongst the host of vehicles like a shark in a school of fish, Cleveland turned speedily parallel parking into a tight spot between a gray Chrysler and an old sky-blue Cadillac. Just then out the corner of my eye I spotted the faint reflection of the van flickering off the luminescent rays of the moon. "Cleveland"! I screamed excitedly snatching him by the shoulder to draw his attention to the immediacy of the situation. Cleveland appeared distracted as he looked down reading numbers off his beeper. "What the fuck nigga"? Looking up Cleveland eyes became transfixed on the source of all my ire. The black van sped up cutting us off as it screeched to a grinding halt. Like rats trapped in a cage me, DJ, Cleveland and Keith scrambled to exit the vehicle. "Lock the doors, I got all my shit in here" Cleveland exclaimed. He was right, Cleveland had money and jewels in the dash, drugs in the trunk and we all had hundreds of dollars' worth of designer clothing in the back seat of the car. The door of Van slid open, Iron and his henchmen slid out the vehicle carrying M-1's, M-16's and a host of other weaponry. With the stealth of a panther they crouched into firing position. Weapon in hand, Iron approached the vehicle cautiously. Cleveland where my bumbo clod money! Iron held the M1 with one hand pointing horizontally, as he swaggered towards the vehicle. Where's my money! Iron cocked his weapon and slapped a 100 round banana clip in the chamber tossing his matted dread locks

175

across the brow of his face. I felt my heart beating in my throat. The world moved in slow motion, as Cleveland hit the automatic locks in the vehicle, we took off running in all four directions. Keith was on autopilot; he took off sprinting. He had leaped over a gate and had run five blocks in 3.5 seconds. DJ had exited the rear left side of the vehicle and had dipped behind two cars. Racing at a low sprint he dashed out of the parking lot and ran between two project buildings quickly disappearing into the night. I was bewildered and confused; I was still exiting the vehicle and had not determined my route of escape. It all had happened so quickly; my reaction time was delayed due to shock and fear. Cleveland exited the vehicle and moved quickly feinting as though he was going to run to the right. As Iron drew his weapon to shoot, Cleveland threw a round house kick knocking the weapon from Irons hand. As Iron scrambled for the weapon Cleveland ran directly towards Iron's two henchmen and executed a flying scissor kick. While the other goons were distracted, I exited the vehicle. I quickly grabbed for an umbrella that rested in the back seat. I was the last to exit the vehicle and came face to face with one of Iron's henchmen who had his weapon trained on me. My body caught on fire, my adrenal response had kicked in; it was either do or die.

I immediately exploded into action. Racing toward my assailant I raised the umbrella welding it like a javelin. Tree-Top, as my assailant was called, was momentarily stunned by my brazen courage as most who have been confronted by gun slinging Rasta's immediately froze, fell to their knees and begged for their lives before being killed. Aiming high I lunged the umbrella propelling it like a spear; the tip of the umbrella struck Tree Top across the bridge of his nose; blood splattered everywhere, momentarily blinding him. Tree Top crumbled to the floor like a deck of cards falling into the fetal position. Diving over his body I took off like an Olympic runner. Iron and his boys had recovered quickly and began dumping machine gun rounds. I ran in a zigzag pattern to avoid getting hit by the shells. Bullets whizzed by my head ricocheting off the gate and sidewalk; sparks flew everywhere. As I ran darkness enveloped me, I saw nothing but the Langston Hughes towers in the distance. My body was warm, my focus unwavering as I sought to reach my destination, for there it was home.

We were fortunate that night everyone escaped without a scratch; we all met in the parking lot of Langston Hughes projects under the cover of darkness. We chose an alternative route to reach Van Dyke Projects that night, once home we assessed the events of the evening. After much contemplation I resolved to divorce the game; I was done. I didn't give a fuck about being the man, rocking jewels, having fly cars, bitches, glory or ghetto superstardom; I wanted to live. I tasted the rewards the streets could give. It was sweet but left a bad taste in my mouth. The next morning, we returned to the parking lot to retrieve our shit from the whip. To our sorrow the car was destroyed; the tires were flattened; the body of the vehicle was riddled with bullet holes; the hood and the ceiling of the car were crushed. Every window was smashed and shattered, and the vehicle was burned, all that remained was a shattered husk; the money, the drugs the clothes were all gone. Was it karma? Was it fate? Was it justice; I don't know, but I wasn't staying around to find out. Mother always said that if good boys did bad shit, they would always suffer the consequences immediately; I wasn't exempt. God spared my life that night I could have been lying dead in the parking lot of the projects had God not watched over me. I heard the message loud and clear. Keith almost lost his life after being beaten almost half to death. Me, DJ, Cleveland and Keith had been shot at, everything Cleveland stole had been lost that night; everything. The message was clear this shit wasn't for me. Never again would my hand touch drugs. The summer was nearing its end. Me and DJ would be returning to school. Cleveland and Keith had long since dropped out. The future was uncertain for them. Maybe they would once again try to fuck with the drug game and take their chances at becoming Dons, or maybe they would wise up and search for more lucrative prospects; however, one thing was certain I would master the game of life and not let life master me.

CHAPTER 17   STICK UP KID

Cleveland took his set back poorly, he wanted to save face. The loss of his car, money, clothes, jewels & drugs severely damaged his confidence and ego. For a time, he had a name in the streets, he had let the illusion of power go to his head. Like a king he had been dethroned falling off his pedestal. No longer could he buy weight in the streets; his name and reputation were fucked up. He was known in the game as a thief; even if he had loot connects wasn't fucking with him on general principle alone; his money was considered no good. He was dead to the streets; Cleveland had violated the code of honor and the system of ethics amongst the criminal underground. Anyone caught supplying Cleveland with product would be as good as dead.

Cleveland played a low profile for almost a year. He vowed he would return to the streets with a vengeance. During his hiatus, he pondered the many aspects of the game; his triumphs as well as his failures. This time around he would be smarter. He would conduct himself like a true business man. He would become a one-man stickup crew. Operating solo he would move in a clandestine manner putting in work in the dead of the night and then disappear like a ghost. If he couldn't be a member of the game, he would change the rules. After much contemplation, he resigned to take a job. Rhonda, Cleveland's girlfriend, had the hook up; she worked in private industry as the director of human resources and had given Cleveland a job working as a maintenance man. Cleveland made eight hundred dollars a week just emptying ash trays and sweeping floors; easy shit; easy money. It was 1989, eight hundred dollars was the equivalent of sixteen hundred dollars. Cleveland could resign from the game and live comfortably. However, the lure of the game beckoned him, the streets had a powerful attraction that Cleveland could not shake. Although he made an excellent source of income with his new job, he had become accustomed to making ten thousand dollars a week while in the crack game. He wasn't accustomed to obeying rules and taking directions from supervisors; he was used to being his own boss. The nine to five rat race was for lame ass square niggas he reasoned. He was used to sleeping all day, smoking weed in the afternoon and slinging rocks all night on the streets. Rhonda wanted the best for her man; she loved him. She knew who he was and what he was into, but she believed she could help him to surpass the game and become a progressive member of society. Cleveland was incorrigible and would never conform to the societal rat race. However, he played the game to the hilt. Cleveland got engaged to Rhonda, got her pregnant and she gave birth to his child. To outside appearances all seemed well. He had everything any man would want a beautiful fiancé, a good job a handsome son and a nice apartment; but he wasn't satisfied he wanted the life; he wanted to be a king pin. He used his job as a front; by day he would dress in blue uniform and would leave for work; by night he would prowl the streets of Brownsville donning a black army suit carrying two sawed off shotguns in search for victims to rob of all their personal possessions.

Cleveland had a penchant for jewelry, with Valentine's Day two weeks away Rhonda had already suggested that she wanted 24 karat heart shaped bamboo earrings. Her gift was inexpensive costing about one hundred seventy-five dollars. Cleveland pondered he could cop that shit at half the price if he went to Delancey Street or to Canal on a Tuesday or Wednesday; the Jews and the Chinese were always hungry to make a sale when business was slow. Cleveland had other shit in mind however, he wanted to get back on; he wanted to shine, he felt invisible in the streets. He wasn't the man no more; niggas weren't giving him the nod as he strolled the boulevard. He couldn't touch hands with the "Big Willies". His name didn't mean shit in the streets. Everyone was saying he fell off. Cleveland however had a plan. He would stack cash with the proceeds from his current job, cop his motorcycle, re-up on his jewels and gear then come summer blow up on niggas and regain his reputation as a true baller. Cleveland led a double life. Rhonda didn't have a clue. The rent, utility bills, cable, clothes food and other bills were paid on time. Rhonda wanted for nothing however had she known that all her necessities of life; the rent; the bills; food everything were paid for with stickup money she would have cut Cleveland the fuck off. Cleveland was no Robin Hood, he robbed from the poor and working class and wanted to be rich.

Cleveland found his mark one afternoon; she was a cute almond eye caramel complexioned dime piece with a fat ass. He spotted her from the second-floor window of his grandmother's apartment as she walked through the projects. Like a doe caught in the underbrush Cleveland approached stealthily like a jaguar about to capture his prey. His body conveyed mixed messages. His eyes signaled he wanted to fuck; his body exuded danger. He swaggered toward Rakia;

she could not read him. Her body tingled in exaltation; she was captivated by a mixture of fear and infatuation. His eyes appeared to look through her. Her vagina got moist. This nigga fine, she thought. However, she knew she could go no further as she was engaged. She would have a little fun, flirt a little, smile and let the nigga down easy, no one feelings would get hurt; she imagined. However, Cleveland was not one who could take no for an answer, he was used to having his way in every arena, today would be no different. His approach was smooth, he strode up beside her reached out with his right hand and gently grasped her left hand. He sized her up quickly; he knew at once she was on his dick. Perhaps he could bag that number, give her a fake name, hit the pussy, and rob the crib while she slept. Rakia was a stickup kids dream; her ears were meticulously adorned with two pair of bamboo hoop earrings. Her hands were ornamented with a variety of rings; she wore two fingered rings and diamond crusted initial rings on three of her fingers on her right hand. Her left hand was decorated with a sparkling diamond engagement ring; a tennis bracelet lit up her wrist. He looked away quickly not wanting to reveal the focus of his attention. In one sweep, he pivoted his body around her one hundred eighty degrees blocking her path. He now stood before her closing the gap. With his left hand he reached forth and gently held her right hand closing the circle. Smiling, Rakia continued to move forward Cleveland led chase moving backward as he smiled licking his lips like he was LL Cool

J. Listen Miss lady I don't want to take up two much of your time; he moved in close smelling the aromatic fragrance of her perfume dance in his nostrils. I couldn't help but notice why a choice young woman would be walking these streets alone, if you were my lady you would turn my house into a home. If I were your man, I would never leave you alone. Rakia moved back placed her hands on her hips as she chewed her gun eying Cleveland from head to toe. You cute and all, but you move like a playa; she eyed Cleveland's package and knew he was packing. No mama I'm not a player but I know what I like. Listen ma, let me cut to the chase, I'm feeling you, maybe one day

I can take you out on a date. Cleveland reached into his pocket and pulled out a fifty-dollar bill and wrote his number on it attempting to place it in her hand. Rakia was tempted to snatch the money out of his hand, but she knew she would have to give up some pussy if he was a live motherfucker; only tricks gave money and gifts for conversation and a smile. Reaching out touching Cleveland's chest Rakia looked Cleveland in his eye shaking her head. "Na boo I got to keep it thorough, you a cute dude playboy but I'm already in a relationship; my man handles his business; I want for nothing as you can see; she turned around with both hands opened wide showing three hundred sixty degrees of her beauty. The smile, charm and finesse which Cleveland initially displayed to draw in Rakia quickly turned into anger. Oh, it's like that, Cleveland grimaced shaking his head up and down. Stepping backward Cleveland broke into a sideways sprint towards the building; all the while staring Rakia straight into her eyes. He would catch her before she hit Blake Avenue he reasoned; the shotgun would do the rest of the work. Cleveland dashed up the stairs taking two steps at time. He slid into is grandmothers dilapidated two-bedroom apartment. His grandmother barely noticed as she lay confined to a wheelchair staring into space in a semi-comatose condition. Cleveland scrambled to retrieve the sawed-off shotgun under the tattered sheets of his mattress. He rushed toward the window eyeing his prey as he loaded the shells cocking the barrel of his shotgun. Rakia continued down the tree lined path oblivious to the impending danger that imperiled her. Within minutes she would reach Blake Avenue and Cleveland would lose the opportunity to strip her of all her jewels. Throwing on a hooded sweatshirt, Cleveland moved in a clandestine manner, slipped out of his grandmother's apartment and preceded down the back stairwell. As he exited the building, he looked both ways scouting the area as though he were on a recon mission. With his adrenaline now flowing Cleveland burst forth from the back of the building like a Cheetah advancing on his prey. Crouching low He ran up the block with his shotgun held horizontally; the butt of the gun resting comfortably on his shoulder. As she neared the corner of the block Cleveland crept up from behind intercepting her. He embraced her with his left hand, with his right he poked her in the ribs with the barrel of the shotgun. Rakia stopped dead in her tracks frozen with fear. Cleveland kissed her on the nape of her neck, his hot breath blowing gently in her ear. You should've given me the play bitch, now you getting played. Rakia was numb, she couldn't talk, her body trembled, and urine ran freely down her legs. Tears began streaming down her face. She looked down as she didn't want to face her victimizer for fear, he might take her life. Cleveland peeled off his baseball cap and held it in his left hand while pointing the shot gun with his right aiming at Rakia's face. "Give me everything; I want your jewels; your rings; your money; your chain; everything. Rakia began to openly sob; makeup and mucus ran down her face. She complied with Cleveland demands and began quickly relinquishing her worldly possessions. She peeled off her rings, her tennis bracelet, and the rings on all her fingers, her necklace, name chain and both pairs of her bamboo hoop earrings. Cleveland stood back and smiled seemingly satisfied with his nefarious deed. However, he was not finished. He pointed the shotgun at Rakia's chest. Open your bra bitch! He knew most females carried the bulk of their stash in their bra as a precaution in case their pocketbook was stolen. Rakia was defeated; he broke her psychologically and physically. She could not raise her head in defiance, she had nothing left. He stripped her of every facet of her dignity. She reached in her bra and placed a wad of cash coiled in a rubber band into Cleveland's hat. "Turn around and walk away", Cleveland tapped her with the shot gun on the back of her head. If you turn around, I am going to blow your head off; don't test me, Cleveland growled. Rakia did as she was instructed. Tears streamed down her face as she crossed Blake Avenue; she was shell shocked. Rakia had a photographic memory; it would serve her well when describing her assailant to her man and then to the police.

After his first string of successful robberies the stickups became a routine. It wasn't the need for cash that compelled Cleveland insatiable desire to possess the materials of others. It was the high that accompanied each take; it was the adrenaline rush that felt sweeter than virgin pussy. It was the fear he derived in others that made him feel powerful. It was the thrill of the hunt that gratified his sociopathic ego. It was for this reason he continued to habitually rob others.

Cleveland gained a name mired in infamy; he reinvented himself. He continued to work while engaged in the stickup game. His wife children and family truly believed him to be the quintessential working man; however, the reality was farther from the truth. Many a night found Cleveland exhausted knocking at the foot of my door. Glistening in sweat, his hands would be laden with various baubles and jewels from his many escapades. However, something was different; those skilled in the stickup game usually liquidated their plunder through cash generated from pawning their jewels. Cleveland on the other hand no longer wore jewels, chains or watches. His appearance began to diminish; instead of looking like a don he began to look like a con. Me & DJ began to distance ourselves from Cleveland. We seldom saw him anymore, when we did the comradery we once felt was gone; we no longer felt comfortable around him. Cleveland no longer smiled and appeared anxious and shifty eyed. His skin was dry, his eyes where reddened & he smelled as though he had not washed in days. His shine was gone and had now been replaced by darkness. Was it karma, were his demons overpowering him, or was it something else. There were many things we hadn't known. Cleveland had now been estranged from his wife Ronda for quite some time due to the difficulties she had faced at his hand. She was abused and was a victim of domestic violence for three years since they had married. She tried her best to hide the tale tell signs of her mistreatment. The black eyes, swollen lips, welts & bruises covering her body were well hidden with shades, hats & makeup. Things began to disappear in her home.

186

T.V.'s, jewelry, money, pocketbooks, often at times, even food from the refrigerator went missing. All the while Cleveland through tearful eyes implored Rhonda of his innocence. In the end Rhonda sought an order of protection and the police removed Cleveland from his home. He later met up with Gloria a dark skinned fifty-two-year-old cougar with a penchant for young flesh. Rumor had it that Cleveland got sprung after Gloria performed fellatio on him for three days straight. From that point on him and Gloria were inseparable. Gloria had mastered the art of seduction and knew how to hold a man. She fed, fucked & sucked Cleveland into submission. To solidify her hold on him she began lacing his weed. Unbeknownst to him Gloria sprinkled rocks of crack cocaine into Cleveland's blunt, for months he remained oblivious to her scheme. Cleveland continued to do stickups; however, he now used the money pawned from his many robberies to line Gloria's pockets. One day after an evening of marathon sex Gloria revealed to Cleveland that she had been lacing his weed with crack for over several months. Gloria explained that she had introduced him to woolies; a mixture of crack and weed, because she thought it would calm his nerves and give him more clarity while outperforming is duties. Gloria peered deeply into his eyes searching the depths of his soul for his response. As he lay in darkness exhausted high and spent from releasing his seed, he shrugged his shoulders and remained indifferent to his plight. He was already house broken; at this point he couldn't give a fuck whether she poked him with a dope needle or placed the spent waste of her menstrual cycle into his spaghetti, he was in love with her ass, mouth and pussy. Cleveland smiled and lunged forward pulling Gloria atop of him. She straddled his dick and began riding him. Cleveland signaled his absolute submission by seizing the woolies from her hand and inhaling deeply as he fell back on the bed in a crack & weed orgasmic bliss. Gloria knew she had Cleveland's on lock. She stood up over Cleveland as he ejaculated and commenced to giving him a golden shower. A stream of piss rained down Cleveland cock. His body shuddered; he had never felt the pleasure this ugly black motherfucker gave him. He was now under her spell. He had lost his wife, his home, his family and his friends and was now a crack head.

News of Cleveland's newfound crack addiction quickly traveled along the grapevine. It wasn't long before Cleveland lost his job as his need to acquire crack made him turn to the stick-up game as a full-time profession. The end came quickly for Cleveland. After robbing over forty people within a six-month period the police had acquired an accurate description of him from dozens of victims and witness's testimony around the neighborhood. On day while walking across a baseball field in the heart of Van Dyke Projects Cleveland found himself surrounded by fifteen detectives. Finding a weakness in the police gauntlet Cleveland rushed forward towards a six-foot eight Irish detective. Dashing to the right he feinted and did a jumping spin out evading the detective, who grunted, swore and fell on his ass. Cleveland ran into the building and sprinted up fourteen flights of stairs with police hot on his trail. With desperation setting in he reached the roof and raced frantically towards the edge; his only means of escape lay in the cold embrace of death awaiting fourteen stories on the sidewalk below. The door of both the front and rear stair well burst open, a platoon of cops spilled out in every direction canvassing the roof with reckless abandon. Cleveland hid under an air vent; the cold wet gravel kissed his skin as he lay face down in the dank smelly darkness. His heart raced frantically; his body shuddered in fear. He prayed silently to God who he knew would not hear his prayers. If only this were a nightmare, if only he would awaken to the comfort of his bed; he would never rob again; he would never take crack; he would return to his family; his wife; his home, however reality had set in; it was over. The sounds of the German shepherds shocked his consciousness. His stomach knotted up, his blood ran cold and his body was numb with fear. Then like an explosion they struck. He was now the prey; hunted cornered, and about to be captured. The dogs burst forth into the damp dark crawl space viciously ripping into his right leg and left thigh. Blinded by the glare of numerous flashlights he covered his eyes and cowered in the fetal position as he was dragged from under the vent by zealous canines. Cleveland began thrashing wildly to escape. He would rather die than to face the indignity of being thrust up manacled and caged like and animal. The blow of the Billy club met the back of his skull his body felt warm as his face met the gravelly pavement. Rolling over he gazed at the sky as the boots, fist and clubs descended on his head and body in torrent after torrent until he lapped into unconsciousness.

CHAPTER 18   CLUBBING IT UP

The sun rose crested and died, children were conceived and were born, the fate of nations were determined in the wink of the creator's eye, but the Ghetto inevitably remained the same. Men were caged, crazed and went to their graves struggling for the fleeting illusions of street fame. Hood stars shined for a time only to have their stars glimmer no more as they breathed their last as their bullet riddled bodies hit the floor. As for me, I was determined to stay free, to do what I wanted to do, and be who I wanted to be. I would not suffer the fate of my Ghetto comrades. I believed God used the lives of men; the poor; the homeless; the addict; the criminal; as examples of how not to live one's life. Cleveland's capture convinced me that the only reward the game afforded was death or incarceration; I wanted neither. I would die an old man surrounded by my progeny uttering blessing with my last breath.

Cleveland wouldn't be seen for another ten years. He was sent to Elmira, one of the hardest upstate penitentiaries in the northeast. Many called it gladiator school, to others it was the "Belly of the Beast". Once swallowed by the system you were digested and excreted back into society. You would either return being the shit, or you wouldn't be shit, there were only extremes no in between. Never again would I be caught in the game. Me & DJ vowed to live our lives to the fullest. I was young handsome and wanted to make bread, get head, shake a leg and not get hit with lead. I was now eighteen, three years had passed, me and DJ had long since dropped out of school and resolved to get our GED. I figured while we went to school at night we could work during the day. Although I had become accustomed to making bread, I could not go back to being a broke ass nigger. We vowed to go legit, get a square ass job and make square ass money. We knew it would be way less than what we were accustomed to, but I would rather live free than be caged with murderers, man bitches and snitches. We copped a two-bit messenger job at $ 4.25 an hour. Me and DJ clamored to get paper, we came up with capers, we hustled during the day as messengers scrambling from uptown, midtown to downtown making our rounds. We would hustle subway tokens. If we had a run from 42nd street to 59th street, we would take off speed walking to our destination and save two tokens; which at that time was worth $1.50. By the close of the day after conducting 30 messenger runs, we would amass $90.00 in tokens and then cash them back at the token booth. The beauty of the job lay in the fact that we were paid off the books and would receive $35.00 per day. By weeks end we would amass $140.00. In addition, from hustling on a good week we sometimes netted at least $250.00 to $300.00 dollars per week; mind you this was 1989, that was good money then. Friday's was always the shit. We learned about the ambiance of New York as messengers and knew all the hot spots and night clubs. After work me and DJ would shop in Greenwich Village because we did a lot of window shopping during the week and already knew the outfit we were going to buy for the weekend. We would cop a lot of club gear, back in those days iron tipped suede shoes with the bows on the top, Doc Martin boots, wine colored Durango boots, flare bottom pants, paisley and polka dot shirts and apple jack hats were the hot shit club kids were rocking on the scene, so we followed suit and got clean. The night scene was flavor. On Fridays we used to frequent a club called Demerara. It was mid-June; you had smooth brothers, ballers, players, Puerto Ricans and beautiful chicks of every color and description inhabiting the lay out. Dems as it was nostalgically called was virtually a candy store; we called it the meat market because it was stocked with legs, thighs, breast and ass. You had wings, ribs and fish in the club; I wasn't fucking with that. I was a hungry motherfucker who enjoyed laying down eating cherry pie; I also enjoyed riding ponies and stallions; I could handle them. From chicken wings to prime rib; if you had game, if you had swagger, if your gear was right and your game was tight, you might go home with a bad bitch that same night. If you were a Mack you might hit a Shorty from the back, if you were slick you might get a chick to such your dick. The scene was mean and not for the lames or those faints of heart. Many scored on the dance floor and got the chance to do the pubic to pelvic dance or fuck some pussy in the reggae room. This club was always dark, the weed was always sparked, and the chicks were always ready for dick; many came to the club panty-less ready to fuck. The DJ was able to intuit the mood of the crowd and act telepathically blending record after record in succession. The crowd was hypnotized as they swayed to the likes of Shaba, Cutty Ranks, Super Cat, Loui Rankin and others. The reggae room was a virtual sweat box that reeked of weed pussy and perfume. The smooth sounds of steel pulse and Soca reverberated as the heart pounding bass of the sound system vibrated the soul. The darkness was dense at times; you couldn't see your hand in front of your face. The room was filled with gyrating bodies moving in unison caught in the rhythmic sway of the African drum. You could wind, grind, rub and suck some titties and press your cock on the panty print of a bitch's vagina if she got moist enough, she would let you slip your dick into her pussy. Lovers caught in the ecstatic embrace of ecstasy pantomimed the symbolic ritualism of sex as the erotic interplay of bodies wiggled, jiggled and grinded in preparation for penetration. This was the life we lived for, the club scene was a place where you could meet a vibrant mix of individuals from all classes and walks of life. It was a melting pot, a mixture of cultures not clashing but harmonizing in a cacophony of rhythms music and dance. The warm summer nights and the hot sweltering days merged like two long lost lovers held in a passionate embrace. As quickly as the sun rose, peaked and set, so to was the summer nearing its end.

CHAPTER 19   LEARNING THE GAME

I was young fresh and living my life. I ran to and ran through bitches. I only had one life live and all my love to give. I wasn't looking for one shorty to lie with and get locked down...feel me. I had a variety of Spanish chicks, a handful of white chicks, and one or two Oriental broads but I was in love with the sisters. That coco-butter brown skin, those luscious hips and caramel lips had me open. They had the lotion to my love potion. However, I knew I had to remain focused because pussy was powerful, it toppled Empires and made kings into weak men. I came up with a formula to keep my shit tight. I was going stick and move, move and stick. I would amass mad telephone numbers from a variety of chicks and throughout the week visit each one of them. I often politicked with the older heads on the science of Macking women. I was told by the OG's to never stay with one woman for too long as bitches had a way of draining your mojo and If you stayed with one for too long, they would eventually figure you out and lose interest.

I liked listening to the meanderings of the old heads. They always presented numerous angels for a nigga to ponder regarding the pussy game. My man Ace, a fifty-year-old player used to school me on the science of female psychology when we chilled in front of the building. You young niggas don't know shit about pussy. He pulled down his skull cap to cover his left eye as he blew billows of carcinogenic vapors from his nostril as he pulled on a cigarette. Let me tell you something, he leaned in close and tugged on my arm pulling me close as to guard his hidden secrets from the ears of the world. Everything you think you know about a bitch is a lie little nigga. He stared at me intently searching my eyes to gauge my level of attention. I was now intrigued like a motherfucker. Ace leaned against the wall and chuckled snapping his finger as if amused with himself, he continued his diatribe. "Listen a bitch always wants what she can't have and what she can't have she'll try to grab. I laughed but the truth of his words was unmistakably deep, I would gain a deeper insight into its meaning as I put his words into practice. Pushing off the wall of the building lobby he moved towards me as if to strike, but not with his fist only his words. Listen young buck, if you give a bitch all your shit, she'll cut you off and hop on another niggas dick. Never tell a bitch you love her, never show emotions of any kind because a bitch is always searching for signs of weakness. You got to be ice cold little nigga, he swaggered around me in circles and smacked me against my chest driving home his point. The colder you get the hotter they sweat. By nature, a woman is naturally inclined to test a man. A woman wants to know what makes a nigga tick. She'll test your strength to see if you pussy or whether your aggressive. She'll play fight with you to test your prowess. She'll try to dominate you, tell you what to do, boss you around. She'll try to get you jealous, by flirting with other motherfuckers; just to see your reaction. She'll try to play mind games to test whether you up on G little nigga. If she can't puppy train you, she'll try to pussy whip you. Watch young buck, trust me on this shit, he intoned. A bitch

195

will try to get you hooked on the pussy. She'll give you all the pussy you want. She let you fuck her in the shower, in the movies, in the bathroom or in any type of strange place. Be careful, because this is the number one weapon in a bitch arsenal-sucking dick. If she can't get your nose open fucking you, she'll try to suck your dick till you come. The most dangerous chick is one who swallows; a lot of playas get check mated with that maneuver and be whooped like a motherfucker ready to wife these chicks. The enormity of his words sunk in my mind like a fresh sponge in dish water. I was intent on soaking up every aspect of the game. Ace moved back and paused in deep thought as though he were pulling the memories of his vast experience like a rabbit out the hat. Look son, Ace said, I been running game on all types of bitches, tall, short, pretty, ugly, smart and dumb as a dip shit but all women have one thing in common. If you beat, eat and treat that pussy like it's a full-time job, they'll give you their money, they'll leave their husbands, they'll even quit their jobs just to get a piece of the dick. Son you must fuck a bitch like she stole something, making love is for bitch niggas in Harlequin Love Novels, fucking is for real niggas. Simply put young nigga, lay dick and don't give a shit. Live by that motto and you'll be the master of your tomorrow.

The advice my man Ace gave me I ran with that shit and started on my full time macking. I met this dark-skinned pretty bitch named Niqua. Her man was locked up on some Federal shit and was doing ten years out west, he left her with all the keys, security codes, bank account numbers and most of all the money. Shorty had a nice spacious loft on Broadway in Williamsburg Brooklyn. I met her on the humble in East New York when I was with my boys in the park playing a little ball. She strolled on the court wearing this pretty yellow sun dress and some yellow and white striped Polo slippers. Niqua was five four thick as day old grits and when she walked her ass jiggled like a bowl of jello; that was going to be my next shorty and I wasn't taking no for an answer. I stepped to her confidently, I had to make sure my game was tight because this was a top notch hotty with a banging body. A lot of pure players was intimidated by this bitch and by the way she carried herself she knew she was the shit. So, I was poised to take her down a notch to let her know that she wasn't all that. I stepped to her, I had no fear, I was going to shoot the gift or crumble like a deck of cards. Walking up beside her I took off my hat and exposed my 360 waves. She looked at me with a slick side eye. With a sarcastic grimace, she stopped and placed her hands on her hips exposing a portion of her voluptuous ass and rolled her eyes like a seasoned Louisiana whore. "Well nigga you going to say something or just stroll with me like a toddler with a pissy pamper. I collected myself, my response had to be swift, sharp and worthy of the player's hall of fame. I went through my mental rolodex of one liners, nothing seemed to apply. Truly this was a unique bitch so 1 had to come up with something fast, I had to think outside the box, I couldn't choke and let this one slide through my fingers. Well my name isn't Todo, but I want to walk with you down the yellow brick road, and thrust me shorty I am shoot the gift, you don't have to go to no wizard seeking nothing. My name is Lasar I'm give you my name and number and I know you going to do what's right, so I'm going to sit back and wait for you to call me tonight. I smiled on the inside, because I knew she was feeling my game. I watched her body language she gave away all the signs attraction; she crossed her legs, she played with her hair and she looked me dead in my eyes. My dick jumped with excitement as I glared at her with x-ray eyes. She peered at me with bedroom eyes and smiled stating, you got A little game, I give you that. I like your style. I thought you were going to come at me on some -Yo Shorty bullshit, but your approach was original, so you get a ten on my score card nigga. I placed my hand on my chin, licked my lips and dipped into my pocket, pulled out a crisp ten-dollar bill folded it down the middle and wrote my name and telephone number. Listen give me a call I got plans for me and you. She eyed me suspiciously with a sly girlish grin, ok cutie we'll link up. She turned and walked away strolling like a stallion. I almost come in my pants. I couldn't wait for the chance to fuck this broad, but I had to play it cool or I would come off looking like a thirsty hound dog. I waited three days before I dropped shorty a line. I spit the game the way it was supposed to be spit and she took a liking to me like a dope feign to a drug. Niqua fell hard for a nigga and she wasn't scared to spend no bread. Every time we linked up, she had mad weed and liquor on deck, we used to go out eat, hit the club and come back to her loft and fuck. I had to hold it down; I knew she was trying to get me open. She was trying to turn me out and turn me into the bitch while she was taking on a more masculine role; paying for everything, tricking hard; sucking and riding dick, but I wouldn't be caught in her web cause game recognize game and I would play this trick bitch to the hilt until the game was over. One evening after a night of hard partying and drinking me and shorty came back to the crib and she approached me on some sideways shit. While she massaged my chest, back and sucked my chest she looked up into my eyes and asked "Ale I need you to do something for me, before you say no, consider what we have and then think hard whether I fuck with you at all. This bitch thought she was slick; I was being primed; all that tricking and fucking and breaking bread with a nigga was done for a reason. I sat up and moved her off me and peered deep into her eyes to read her soul. She moved closer to me and began blowing sweet kisses into my ear. She whispered "baby I have a certain lifestyle I need to uphold. When my man was home, I was a kept bitch, I didn't have to work, and I didn't want for nothing. My man had the money on deck, I had my shoe and my bag game on deck, my hair and my nails were always tight, and I kept at least a grand on me just on general principle; that's how my nigga fucked with me.... feel me! I peeped this bitch she was passionate about what she was saying and how she felt. The average nigga would have fell for her gift of gab, but I got schooled by cold hearted players, ballers and pimps. I would not let this bitch turn me into her flunkey trick nigga...fuck that. I watched her body language, she talked with her hands and her mouthpiece was slick; shorty was a Mack ho, a Donnette and a straight up alpha female. She stepped to me and took me by the hand. "Look boo I'm a keep it one hundred, I need you to move some shit for me. I moved in closer and sat beside her and lifted one eyebrow sarcastically. Cutting to the chase, I cut her short in mid-sentence. Listen stop bullshitting me and say what you have to say. All right nigga if you want to keep fucking this bomb ass pussy you going to have to move some weight, transport some coca, yayo, girl, china white, understand! Niqua was well versed at manipulating men, I had not been the first motherfucker she seduced into being a drug mule, but I would not be the next spider caught in this bitch's web. I wasn't one of those niggas that valued pussy over everything. I had seen how my cousin used to ball-out when he was in the game. I had also seen him fall-off when he got on crack and later get locked the fuck up; I would not be that guy. I looked Niqua dead in her eyes and stood up quickly and held her by her chin. "Look shorty I'm feeling you, the pussy is the bomb and we had some good times together, but I'm not carting shit around. I got a lot to lose, my life, my freedom, my family, that's important to me and I'm not willing to risk that for nothing so I guess it's a wrap. Her face deceptively masked with a look of love and passion quickly turned into that of anger. I walked towards the door and she followed behind me screaming obscenities. "Alex, I knew you was a bitch ass motherfucker. Get the fuck out my house you motherfucking pussy ass nigga. She snarled at me, her mask had fallen, and her true personality was revealed. You will never get another whiff of this pussy motherfucker; she smacked on her ass and tapped her pussy twisting her fingers upward while rolling her eyes and sucking her teeth. I moved quickly to the door and was out, never to return. It was another lesson learned; another experience gained. I would never trust a big butt and a smile. The old saying was true all that glittered was not gold and what looked good wasn't always good for you.

CHAPTER 20   BECOMING CONSCIOUS

I learned many lessons in my dealing with the opposite sex; they were not to be trusted. However, I would not dwell on my past relationships and let them weigh me down. I had too many bitches to fuck and money to get. I had to get my shit together physically and mentally. I had to get my mind right. I prayed to the Highest to give me clarity of mind that I may find purpose, my prayers were finally answered. I was 19 and full of questions. I got the game from the streets, but I now pondered the mysteries of life. I had always been naturally inquisitive. I wondered how the world came to be, how life was structured, why were there some who had everything while others had next to nothing. I wanted to know what operative force governed the world, who was in charge and how did they acquire their power. I began to touch base with June my mother's ex-husband. It had been almost 9 years since we last spoke, but I felt compelled to see him. He had now lived in Tilden Projects; June had never lived on his own, he was a master manipulator of women, he lived with them most of his adult life. He was an old school player, with little book smarts but a PHD in streetology. Tilden had not changed one bit; it was every bit as grimy as I remembered in my youth. I came to 285 Livonia Avenue. Hood niggas gathered in groups of 20 in front of the building. The light in the elevator was out and the floor was inundated with beer and urine. I held my breath as I ascended the shaft of this iron crusted tomb. The elevator reached the twelfth floor. I knocked on the door, I still felt tinges of anxiety as I was facing a man whom I feared the whole of my childhood; however, I would face my fears and stand before him as a man face to face. The door opened; I was bombarded by the overwhelming scent of incense masking a hint of marijuana. June approached the door, he had gotten fat, his skin was darker than I remembered; I heard he was using boy, aka p-funk also known as heroin. He looked me in my eyes, once again the fear gripped me, but I put on my game face, he would never know he still had power over me. "Well come in nigga you just going to stand there with that dumb look on your face. "I came in the house was neatly decorated and spotless a strong indication that he did not live alone. Sabrina, the lady of the house came out the back room. She was a pretty coco-brown heavy-set middle-aged woman with streaks of grey in her hair. She offered me something to drink, I accepted. I followed June to the living room, we sat, and he began to tell me about his childhood how his father was illiterate drunk who beat his mother but was a good provider as he worked in a factory. I had concluded that everything that he had become was a result of his childhood. He had become the image of his father a man who was mean and heartless. Like many of the Black men in those days he was strong silent and stoic, he never displayed any emotions, he never showed love, it was not considered manlike behavior.

It all made sense; memories of my childhood came flooding back into my consciousness. June's father had taught me how to tie my shoes, hang up my clothes, make a bed and fold my clothes; I had learned these lessons while under a state of terror. I remember distinctly while learning to fold clothes, June's father would demonstrate the proper technique only once, and you dare not ask questions for you would get smacked in your mouth. You only had one time to learn and master what was being taught, any mistake would result in an ass whipping. I was under heightened pressure to learn. I was under extreme stress, every mistake, every misstep, I was screamed at, cursed out and beaten; under these circumstances I learned quickly. I sat and listened while June recalled the memories of his turbulent past, his brutal relationship with his father and how it resulted in him engaging in juvenile delinquent behavior, drug use, joining gangs and being institutionalized. This influenced his relationships with all his women. Psychologically he had become just like his father; angry; mean; abusive; possessive and controlling. He believed that he had no control in the world surrounding him. However, in his household he would be master and king of his dominion even if he had to beat his kids and his woman into submission. I now began to understand how pathological behaviors like crime, drug abuse, poverty, teenage pregnancy, domestic violence and a host of other ills could be passed from one generation to another like a disease. The fear had infected me as well. I was conflicted…I hated, feared and loved this man for he was the only father I knew. He was the only other male example in my life besides my grandfather. Why was he telling me these things I pondered, perhaps it was time for me to understand certain truths, perhaps it was time for the veil to be lifted from my eyes so that I could awaken and understand the real world.

He looked into my eyes as he sat spread eagle toking on a Bamboo cigarette stuffed with marijuana. Nigga I need you to understand my story. I didn't bring you here just to rap about bullshit motherfucker. It ends now...now! I brought you here to end the cycle. Look at me...look at me! I raised my eyes from the floor and gazed upon the man I feared since my childhood. He sat slumped in a weed and heroin induced stupor nodding in and out of consciousness as he paused between his words. He opened his blood shot mucus crusted eyes and began to speak. Son I'm 59 years old, I have a six-grade education, I been in and out of jail for most of my life. I have shot, cut and beaten men, even tried my hand at pimping. I have robbed, stolen and been abusive to women. Son who I am is a curse passed down to me by my father and his father before him. I am an heir to a legacy of ignorance. All my life I was a street hustler, a nigga and a womanizer. Look at me son.... I aint shit!!! It's too late for me.

But you still have a chance to redeem yourself to break this curse. I sat dumbfounded and bewildered. What was he trying to tell me speaking of curses and being and heir to a legacy of ignorance? I moved in closer because I wanted to understand the depth of what he was trying to convey. He stood up pointed his finger at me and stated: "this shit it didn't start with me nor my father". He paused to gage the depths his words were having on me. He looked at me deeply, his gaze burned a hole in my soul. He inhaled deeply on his joint and exhaled billows of vaporous smoke; it was as if his soul had left his body. June smiled and slowly sat back into his chair and looked up to the heavens as though he were trying to grasp the enormity of each word. He slowly turned looked at me and began to speak. "Our people were the first people on the Earth. We are the Original man and woman; our people are millions of years old; older than the Bible or the Koran. In ancient times we inhabited every part of this planet. We built cyclopean megalithic structures throughout the earth. We observed and mapped the stars, invented mathematics; writing, astrology and astronomy. We created the first civilizations in Africa, Asia, North Central and South America. While the White man languished in the caves and mountains of Europe walking on all fours and eating raw flesh, we were kings and Queens and erected temples ornamented in gold, we were worshipped as Gods by the rest of mankind. Our civilization lasted over 100 thousand years. We are the mother and fathers of civilization. We gave the world law, agriculture and the calendar. We civilized the savages and they repaid us with treachery. The Asians and the Europeans came wave after wave invading our kingdoms killing, burning, pillaging, raiding, destroying and later occupying our lands. For six thousand years Africa remained under siege by the Persians, the Assyrians, the Romans, the Greeks, the British and the Arabs until our kingdoms were destroyed. Our people were sold into captivity and taken from our ancestral homeland in Africa. We were transported to North America, South America and the Caribbean. We were stripped of our names, languages, religions and culture. Our family bonds were broken our tribe names were forgotten. We were sold into captivity and enslaved for 400 years. We became chattel, we became property like a table or chair. We were treated less than human, under the Constitution we were classified as 3/5ths of a human being. They renamed us, they called us niggers, negro, colored & black. We suffered through slavery, the Black Codes, Jim Crow apartheid, lynching & segregation. We still suffer the effects of racism and discrimination to this very day…and why, because we don't have knowledge of self. We don't know who we are and where we came from. We suffer from cultural amnesia, because of this our families are broken, our neighborhoods are overrun with crime, gangs, poverty, drugs and death. Son we have been in this fallen state for 16 generations. For many of us the slums, crime the ghetto, death and poverty have become a way of life. We have become functionally dysfunctional. I listened in stunned silence; never had I heard the true story of my people. I was only exposed to his-story. I only knew that Columbus sailed the ocean blue in 1492 and that Martin Luther king had a dream, but my history was a mystery.

As June continued to speak the veil which had closed my eyes had been lifted, the chains which shackled my mind had been broken and my third eye which had long been closed was now wide open. I had a million questions that I needed answered in one sentence, but I didn't know how to verbalize my newfound consciousness. I sat before June teary eyed unable to speak. June stood up and motioned for me to follow him into the living room. My heart began to beat, why was I fearful? The veil of ignorance had just been lifted from my mind and I was now being led into the light of truth like an initiate carried into the halls of knowledge. I was comfortable in my ignorance like a sleeping man to his bed and like a dead man in his grave, but the light of knowledge awakened me from my sleep and the light of truth raised me from the dead. June lead me to the living room and reached into a huge bookshelf. He extracted two books the Bible and the Quran. "Son these are the two books that started me on my journey to understanding myself". "But understand this youngster, everyman has a path that God patterns specifically for him, each man's path is unique. This library is my treasured jewels, from it you may freely partake and enrich yourself; it is my gift to you. His library was huge; the bookshelf covered two walls. All the book titles were in alphabetical order. I skimmed over his large array of titles from science, astrology, social studies, American history but most of all African history. He had titles from scholars such as J. A. Rogers, John Henrik Clarke, Joseph Ben Jochannan, Ivan Van Sertima, Cheik Ante Diop, WEB Dubois, Malcolm X and many others. I had never heard of these historians; however, these were giants in the field of Black history. I reached forth and began to browse; my hand was magnetically attracted to a small hard cover book entitled "From Superman to Man by JA Rogers.

I had an insatiable quest to find wisdom, but little did I understand that which I was seeking had always been in me. I become a zealot for knowledge. The truth had opened my eyes; however, it was a gift and a curse. It made me angry to walk about the ghetto and see the conditions that Black people were burdened with. Blacks were suffering from post-traumatic slavery disorder; the drugs, gangs' mental illness, incarceration, the broken families, the crime, these were all throw backs from slavery. My studies revealed that in order to truly control a people its men must be destroyed, its women subjugated, its children mis-educated. I saw the long-term effects of slavery and discrimination. I was witness to the toll it took on the Black community. I was conscious but how could I awaken others who were fast asleep. Many times, I felt alone in possession of this knowledge, many times when trying to convey the information about our history and our greatness, people would immediately change the subject, walk away, shun you or make a mockery of the information you brought forth. I attended every Black lecture; I wore African medallions, beads, kente cloth, dashikis and cowrie shells. I divorced myself from American culture and immersed myself in everything Black. I wanted to know every aspect of Black culture. I studied Swahili, I studied Egyptian hieroglyphics, I studied the various kingdoms in Africa; Egypt; Nubia; Cush; Ghana; Mali; Shanghai; Zimbabwe, Timbuktu and Monopatapa. I studied the Trans-Atlantic Slave Trade, Antebellum Slavery, the Black Codes and Jim Crow apartheid yet something was missing. I prayed to God and the ancestors for clarity, vision and the path I needed to walk. One night I dreamed I stood surrounded by tall beautiful Black men and women arrayed in white linen on the Banks of the Nile River. An elder walked towards me and pointed to the water and bade me to drink. I immersed my hand in the Nile and drank and immediately I was possessed with the spirit of my ancestors. I awoke from my dream and immediately knew my purpose. I would awaken those who were asleep; those Black men and women who knew not who they were; those who called themselves niggas and bitches. I would speak to those who the world called invisible; the voiceless, the powerless, those living in poverty. I would tell them of their past greatness. I would tell them they were the Kings and Queens, scientist, mathematicians, builders, explorers and warriors who created Kingdoms, mapped the stars, created edifices in stone, traveled the seas; trotted every part of the earth; created universities and drafted moral codes that men still adhere to till this day.

CHAPTER 21 THE STRUGGLE

I hit the pavement running. I politicked with brothers from the Nation of God and Earths, the Israelites, Muslims, Kemites, Rasta's, Pan Africanist, players, ballers, thugs and everyday brothers. I wanted to absorb the best of every philosophical discipline and be a proselyte to none. My new religion was knowledge, understanding and wisdom and I would blend the best of every discipline into one philosophy based on truth. My goal was to be a free thinker as those who became converts to religious and spiritual ideologies became close minded. In order to unite the global African family, I would have to be able to move freely amongst those from all disciplines and cultural backgrounds. I linked up with one shorty, she was my first disciple. Her name was Daveen. I met shorty at the car show at Jacob Javits convention center. I shot the gift, dropped the jewels, got the digits and bagged her up. She was tall dark skinned and had long Indian hair. She told me she had Cherokee and Seminole in her bloodline but at the end of the day whitey still looked at all of us as niggas. Daveen was a sexy Gemini freak in the sheets and a lady in the streets; she was classy and carried herself like a Queen. She was well versed on all the trendy spots and cultural centers in the city; we hit all the art galleries and lounges and underground upscale parties. She worked for the department of parole and she tricked bread and gave good head. She was an asset to my team, if you know what I mean. She had her own crib and wanted me to move in, but I didn't want to ruin a good thing. I wasn't ready to be captured and locked down by a broad; I liked coming and going as I pleased. I used to come to the crib, we smoked weed, fucked and had numerous cypher session about religion, spirituality, Afrocentricity and philosophy. I gave Daveen mental orgasm and she gave me physical orgasms. After opening her mind, she opened her legs and her mouth giving me orgasmic bliss. She began to worship me; I became her personification of God in the flesh. I rescued her, and I raised her from a state of mental death. She was once deaf, dumb and blind but I enabled her to see the world through her third eye. This was a regular hood chick that used to do coke, drink forties and smoke weed. But after receiving the lessons she removed the weave from her hair, went natural, begin to dress and adorn herself in Afrocentric attire. She stopped smoking weed, changed her diet and became vegan. My shorty went through a complete metamorphosis. Truly this chick was my warrior Queen and she was down to ride with me to hell and back I had no doubt Daveen had my back.

I was a warrior scholar and was thirsty to impress upon the world my new-found consciousness. I conversed with thugs, OG's both young and old as well as those in different states of consciousness. Some were open to receive knowledge of self, some weren't. I brushed my shoulders off and wiped the dust off my feet, for I learned to never cast my pearls to swine and expel unnecessary energy imparting knowledge to those who were unworthy to receive it. I hatched a plan to awaken the masses by producing tracks on African history and various Afro historical facts because spreading the knowledge from mouth to ear was a very slow process. I had to plant seeds in Harlem, East New York, Brownsville, Bed-Stuy and wherever the brothers dwelled in

211

mass because the time for awakening was now. Whatever I was to do it had to be big. It had to touch the lives of as many people as humanely possible in a short period of time. I wanted to open the hearts and minds of my people as the seed of truth had to be planted for the next generation.

The Gods and the ancestors answered my prayers, the opportunity which I sought materialized before my eyes. A minister from the nation of Islam called for a gathering of a million Black youth to meet in Harlem. The last time and event of this proportion took off was in 93 during the Million-Man march in DC. I would not miss this event; this was my time to shine for my people and vibe with the Afrocentric community. The event was Saturday, the media launched a full-scale anti-Black propaganda campaign against the Minister stating he was riling up the youth to attack the police and launch attacks on white people. Those in the conscious community knew this was bullshit, the media goal was to try and persuade the Black masses not to attend the rally fearing that it would explode into violence. But the Black Community came out in mass. Me and Daveen reached 116th by one o'clock, the streets were packed. Never had I stood amongst so many beautiful and diverse Black people. The Bloods, the Crips, Rastas, Kemites, Nuwabians, Five Percenters, Muslims, Africans from the continent, hood rats, thugs and street cats were there, and they all dwelled in peace. The vendors were selling incense, oils, kente cloth, vegan and vegetarian food, CD's and drums. The whiff of roast corn, cabbage, peas and rice, chicken, jerked, BBQ, roasted and grilled filled the air. One would have thought that this was the open market in Ghana or perhaps Senegal, but no this was Harlem...the Mecca and I was there.

This was not a protest march but a rally to call forth Black people from every corner of Black society to meet and discuss issues that affected our daily lives. The venue would be a meeting place to network, converse, meet, greet, focus and reflect on what strategies the community could employ to combat police brutality, racism and discrimination. The minister along with a number of activist and grass roots organizers would address gang violence and a host of other ills that often lead to our youth being incarcerated, dead or marked as felons and forever disenfranchised from American mainstream society. Daveen and I entered the square; an enclosure cordoned off with barriers and an excessive amount of police emergency vehicles, cops, horses and Hercules task force personnel. We were penned in like sheep on all four sides. Should anything jump off we would be ripe for the slaughter. This was the exact reasoning I cancelled my journey to the Million Man March in DC. It was a warrior's instinct to be prepared for any contingency, and my spider sense was tingling. I conducted a visual scan of the area and scoured the faces and badge numbers of the nervous and over vigilant Police officers on the grounds. Helicopters hovered overhead and laid stationary suspended in mid-air. Employing my peripheral vision, I examined the roof tops of the buildings encircling the square. My eyes caught a glimpse of the sun reflecting off the shimmer of glass on the roof top. I squinted and zeroed in on the object of my perception, my heart froze. It was a police officer crouched with a high-powered sniper rifle. I turned north; officers lay in position in the building directly in front of the podium. I looked east they were in position; I looked west, officers stood like sentinels with rifles slung on their shoulders communicating through walkie talkies and headsets. The police were conducting counterinsurgency operations on site and they were well prepared. I grabbed my queen from behind and pulled her close wrapping my left hand around her waist and whispering in her right ear. I gently tapped the bottom of her chin imploring her to look up. "Baby we're surrounded". She looked around quickly her body stiffened, and her eyes widened like saucers. She shifted turning her body around confronting me face to face. "Lasar this is real, this is not a dress rehearsal, we're involving ourselves in some real revolutionary shit...baby I'm scared. I held her closely and consoled her in my arms. "Baby we have prepared ourselves to do the will of the ancestors, don't worry we are protected, but in case an emergency arises, and we find ourselves separated, I want you to meet me at 116th street and Frederick

Douglas Boulevard. She looked me in my eyes, no longer did I sense her fear, for it had be replaced by will and determination. She smiled kissing me on my neck. "For the ancestors", for it is on their shoulders we stand". She clenched and raised her beautiful black fist and cried...Black Power...Black Power.... Black Power!

I became energized, the spirit of fear had disappeared. We moved forward with our mission to build, network, reach and to teach. We ran into members of the communist party, we shared information with brothers from the New Black Panther Party, we brushed shoulders with Nuwabians, shared literature with Hebrew Israelites and brothers who studied metaphysics. It was an electrifying scene, there were

Moors, Kemites, Garveyites, Pan-Africanist, Civil Right activist and Black people of every philosophical persuasion. We distributed almost a thousand pamphlets and politicked with brothers on almost a thousand philosophical platforms regarding how to liberate our people. We all were one body, yet we were divided along ideological lines, we all wanted the same thing, yet we all took various roads and paths to get to our destination. If we could all just be of one mind, one body we could move forward as one people having one aim and one destiny.

Now that we were both cognizant of the police presence in our mist, me and Daveen continued to keep an eye on the opposition and they watched us as well; there were Cops surveying the crowd from windows as well as rooftops with binoculars and other high-tech surveillance equipment. As the people milled about networking, vending, socializing and conversing, an alarm began to resound over the audio system erected on the stage podium. A hush came over the crowd, fifty members of the Fruit of Islam marched in unison. They were magnificently arrayed in black tailored uniforms trimmed in gold and moved as one body. All that could be heard was their steps as they marched in perfect rhythmic motion. They parted the ocean of people assembled in the square like the red sea as they strolled forward towards the stage. As they neared the stage each member of the FOI stopped did a pirouette and turned towards the crowd in perfect formation forming a phalanx. In unison they raised their fist in the Black Power salute as the minister arrived on the podium. The people applauded; their voices resembled the sound of many waters. The thunderous applause continued for several minutes and abruptly ceased as the

215

minister began to speak. The crowd laid entranced as the minister began his powerful discourse denouncing the system of White Supremacy. His oratory was magnificent, his speech was eloquent. He outlined, uncovered and unveiled the hidden agenda the government was systematically employing to control, alienate, oppress and destroy the masses of Black people. The minister spoke truth to power and his words were cutting like a double edge sword. The cops were agitated and fidgety, their faces were red as beets. They gritted their teeth as the minister's words penetrated their lifeless souls. Their eyes spoke volumes, I could see their murderous intentions, however the minister would not reach martyrdom, for in death he would be elevated to a God.

As the minister spoke the crowd roared to a deafening crescendo crying Black Power; Black Power; Black Power. The feeling was electrifying for it had been the first time in my life I felt a part of one family, one people, one nation. The Gods and Earths, the Rastas, Kemites, Israelites, Nuwabians, Muslims, Bloods and Crips became one family. I lost my individuality and became one with masses of my people. I experienced an almost trancelike euphoria, at that moment I began to shed tears of joy, pain and exultation. I quickly turned away from my Queen for it was taboo for her to see me cry, for as a man I had to uphold the banner of power and never display fear or emotion as not to appear weak. I was quickly jarred back to my senses as a flying bottle crashed against the helmet of one of the mounted officers almost knocking him from his horse. He quickly recovered and galloped in the direction of the thrown projectile. Dozens of people were trampled by the horse in the ensuing chaos. Throngs of people began to scramble in every direction. Women screamed in utter panic as they scrambled to protect their children huddling behind cars. This is all the cops wanted, a reason, a justification to employ a murderous crackdown on the assembly of Blacks who gathered peacefully. The cops launched into action and began to close in with shields and batons prominently displayed. The minister tried to implore the crowd to remain calm, but the damage had already been done. The cops moved in and began to beat, drag, subdue and arrest everyone within arm's length. We launched our escape strategy as planned me and Daveen ran and dipped under a tractor trailer, jumped over three police barriers and hauled ass for two blocks to the nearest train station. Surprisingly she was a soldier, she didn't slow down, she didn't falter. I had a newfound respect for my Queen as I knew she would ride for me like a motherfucker. We ran to the rear of the train platform and entered the dark tunnel winding a way along the narrow train platform. It was as if the underworld had awaited our arrival and the darkness embraced us in its icy grip. We moved swiftly until we neared an emergency exit faintly lit by a 40-watt light bulb. There was no room for indecision, I had to create an alternate route for I was sure the next station was crawling with cops searching for those who escaped the ensuing melee. I threw my body full force against the door, pain shot through my shoulder reverberating down my back. The door gave way slightly, I began kicking with one; then both legs all to no avail. The door had not been opened it appeared in over 40 years. Then suddenly the door gave way, I fell forward striking my left side on a stairwell. I looked up and saw a dim ray of sunlight

217

emanating from a sidewalk grill. Cautiously we moved forward up the dim dusty stairwell until we reached the upper level. As we neared street level, I pushed against the grate exhausting all my strength and was able to lift the stainless-steel covering. Clasping both hands together I implored Daveen to step into my hand. I lifted her upwards, she slipped through the opening and rolled onto the sidewalk. She reached down, I backed up allowing myself room for momentum. Backing with both hands against the wall I propelled myself forward running up the 7-foot enclosure and launched off the wall grabbing Daveen's hand. She screamed as the full weight of my body violently threw her off balance. She fell forward and nearly tumbled back into the hole. Grasping her forearm, I scrambled up the hole and rolled on top of her. We laid on the sidewalk momentarily heaving with exhaustion. I jumped to my feet dusted the soot off my garbs turned my shirt backwards. Daveen took off her headwrap, her green black and red beaded anklet and bracelet, tied her ankle length dress tightly around her thighs and we dipped into the crowd and vanished. After returning home that evening I watched the evening news it was reported that there were almost two hundred arrest at the rally, dozens were injured, the minister was arrested for inciting a riot. The news showed soundbites of the minister crying for those at the rally to defend Black women and children. Those at the rally responded and fought valiantly to repel the riot police who used tear gas and pepper spray to disperse the crowd. I learned a valuable lesson that day, as Black People if we have an agenda, we cannot broadcast our plans to our enemies for they will contain and check mate our protest rallies and political movements. Our moves must remain secret, our plans must be executed and only the result of our actions must be seen not the strategies used to employ them. I vowed from that day to move in silence for the revolution could not be televised, the movement had to be clandestine and underground for it to grow. I would remain that gorilla in the bush, strong but hidden among the undergrowth of leaves awaiting that moment to pounce and deliver the killing blow to my enemies.

CHAPTER 22 THE AWAKENING

It was 4AM I was restless, I laid drenched in sweat peering into the darkness at streetlights reflecting from the ceiling. My mind played tricks on me as spirals of purple danced before my eyes. I spoke silently to the Gods petitioning them to answer my prayers. What was the meaning of my life, I contemplated? The only thing in the world that remained constant was change. I continued to educate myself and seek enlightenment in search of that one transformative principle that would aide in my evolution. Me and Daveen parted ways, she was in my life for only a season, for in every experience remained a lesson. What was the moral of my story, what was the message? How was I to take meaning from everything that happened thus far. I was now 25, I was at the crossroads in my life. I could do anything, go anywhere be anything...but what...who...where? These were the unknowns that could only be answered by myself. God knew the answers but remained curiously silent. I continued to date but found no fulfillment in sexual conquest. I was searching for something, a path undiscovered, a road not trod, precipice not reached. I vowed to return to school, to get a square secular education. I had attained street knowledge, I knew various elements of the game, I acquired knowledge of self and politicked with grassroots organizations, I understood the game, I knew how to Mack bitches and get pussy. I had reached the prime of my life and there was no other place to go but up.

I had realized that everything that occurred in my life began and ended with me. Every event that I had experienced was a lesson. Each lesson that I endured made me examine my strengths as well as my weaknesses. Life was preparing me; I was being transformed into a man of character. I should have been dead or in jail and yet I was here. I was strong, I had overcome numerous obstacles; the gangs the drug trade and incarceration. I had seen many of my friends die, many had succumbed to the lure of the ghetto and their lives were changed forever. The insane asylums, graveyards and penal institution all attested to this fact. I was still standing, fortunately many of my counterparts who lived this ghetto experience bore testimony to the insanity of the streets. They sat in wheelchairs; bodies torn by bullets meant for others but finding their mark on them as they were victims of karmic consequences the penalties of which they now bore.

In a forest of decisions how would I plot my path. I vowed not to be like those whom I saw; the forgotten those who got lost, those who have given up. I would strategize, plot and scheme to launch my plans into fruition. I now realized that no one owed me shit. I had to stand up on my own two feet and do it on my own. Regardless of how others claimed they had your back and supported you no one really gave a damn about you, you had to sink or swim. There were only winners and losers and the latter no one recognized, while the former everyone loved. I would no longer tell others of my plans and movements for their envy and jealousy would be the killer of my dreams. No longer would I talk about it, I would be about it. As I pondered my life, I even thought about settling down with one woman, having

221

some babies and living a square life. That's what responsible men did when they reached a certain age. But who would I choose to be my wife, a woman of character or a bubble butt dime piece; these were the decisions that life unfolded before me? I was still young, but I knew time waited for no man. The first thing I had to condition was my mind. Second, I had to eliminate all my bad habits; chiefly procrastination and laziness. These were the most powerful as once they set in you had to employ all your willpower and determination to break free of them.

I had to begin to think outside the box if I wanted to get a different result. I lived a ghetto experience where, poverty, fear, stress, and anger were as normal as breathing. Had I become desensitized to my suffering. Was pathology a normal part of my daily function. What would It be like to accomplish my dreams and become self-sustaining fulfilling role as a man, father, husband and responsible member of my community? For too long I lived amongst those whose dreams had never been fulfilled and talents never recognized. I lived amongst a people who feared success and hated anyone striving to become great. I lived in a world where disfunction was the norm and functional human beings where an anomaly. My eyes were opened, I realized after tasting the forbidden fruit of knowledge that there was a world, I was not a part of, a world I was excluded from. I lived in segregated space, I lived in the Ghetto, a place marked for undesirable populations. It was a prison with invisible walls; the bars were mental the cage was ignorance. The gate keepers were the police, the system, institutions, agencies and economics. I would no longer be bound by ignorance, fettered by stereotypes, and frozen by fear of the unknown. I was free I had been enlightened. My harsh experience as a youth gave birth to the man I was now becoming. There was nothing I could not achieve, no goal was too lofty, there was no glass ceiling, no chasm to wide for me to breach. It was only my own fears, doubts and indecision that kept me bound and imprisoned in the walls of my mind. In a sea of ignorance, I would become an oasis of knowledge unto myself.

I began to understand that everything that occurred in my life happened as a result of the choices I made. Each choice be it small or large created a domino effect in my life and others arounds me. For every action there was an equal and opposite reaction and for every because there was an effect. Like a stone being thrown in into a still pond it causes ripples throughout the pond from the point where it was dropped. The same happens in life of those who live in the hood. We experience a shared commonality confined in the bowels of the ghetto. Although my story was unique, the elders, the teens and many of the youth lived this shared experienced. Our lives converged and intersected through violence, incarceration, death, poverty, fear and the everyday struggle to survive. I was not alone in this journey, yet I felt alone in my understanding of the various factors that contributed to the pathologies our people endured. I knew that along this path I chose to undertake, there would be pitfalls, obstacles and traps laid by the enemies of my people; those within as well as outside the community. I began to understand that the outside world played a powerful effect on those who lived in these chocolate cities. We were affected by microeconomic and sociopolitical forces such as the police, schools, the job market, religious institutions and the family. We were also are affected by macroeconomic forces such as the courts, laws, race, class, and affiliation to historical oppressed minority groups who are impacted by systematic racism as well discrimination. These forces played a powerful part in controlling the lives of those born in the ghetto. How would I navigate this maze of chaos and complexity where few have trod and successfully traveled? I had seen the results of those who lost their way, many went mad after reaching that dead end as they knew not how to reverse course and find another route. Many succumbed while on their journey and chose to escape through alcohol and drugs abuse. While others gave up and journeyed no more; they laid in alleyways sleeping in their own piss and excrement dreaming of bygone days and lost dreams. Those few who were fortunate to navigate the matrix and exit its bowels would not reveal the path taken to reach the other side, nor would they reach back grasping the hand of their brethren who roamed blindly in their mist. I on the hand had a plan. I would not roam blindly through the darkness; I would carry a torch and that torch would be knowledge.

I awoke. Tears fill my eyes, I tried to stand but my body would not cooperate. It was daytime, I could neither tell whether it was morning or noon as my vision was impaired. Father, cried Alexis, thank God you have awakened, you tossed and turned all night crying out Carpe diem, Carpe diem, what does that mean? I laid shocked as I looked upon the face of this beautiful tall woman who addressed me by this title and immediately the memories came flooding back into my consciousness like a dam that had suddenly been broken. I laid in hospice. My body, mature with age, was preserved by intravenous fluids fed through my bloodstream by tubes delicately attached to every extremity. Was I near death? Was my life flashing before me? Was I standing at the edge of eternity and viewing receipts of my life before judgment day? I opened my mouth to speak but could not give voice to my thoughts for what appeared to be an eternity. My voice broke forth like a whale rising from the depths of the deep. Mustering forth all the power in my voice I cried, "Carpe diem means seize the day…seize the day! Although I laid incapacitated my words moved through the room touching the souls of all who were present. My sons, daughters, grands and greatgrandchildren stood before me looking upon me with respect and adoration. They were doctors, nurses, engineers, artist, clergy men and teachers and it was I who touched their lives impressing upon them morals, values, ethics and ideals.

I awakened to a deep state of remembrance; my thoughts flooded my consciousness. I remembered falling into a coma after having a stroke. For 9 years

I remained unconscious in a comatose state. Yet I recalled with vivid clarity every aspect of my life, it was as if each facet of my existence played out like chapters from a movie and I viewed on the sidelines as a silent witness.

As I laid in a state akin to death, I journeyed through the spirit world guided by my ancestors. I was witness to all my mistakes, misfortunes, the good, the bad, the hurt I inflicted on myself and the harm I had caused others. At the lowest point in my life they were there standing beside me holding me up, so I did not fall. With my spirit eyes I saw all the traps placed by my enemies meant to ensnare me. I was blessed to have made it this far, for I saw fields covered with the blood of those who cried from the ground and traps laid

225

to bind the bodies and souls of men. Yet each time I faced eminent death they interceded on my behalf; these beautiful men and women arrayed in white had a purpose for me. For it would be I who would end the cycle of dysfunction and pathology that occurred generation after generation within my family. For it was ignorance that gave birth to fear, hatred, poverty and death. It was I who was made to drink from the river of knowledge and gaze at a reflection of my true self. I broke the generational curses inflicted on my family resulting from slavery, miseducation and segregation. I married, had a prosperous life, reared strong sons and daughters who were educated, ambitious and bright. They in turn gave birth to grandsons, granddaughters and great grands. What was told to me by my father regarding the greatness of our people I bestowed upon each of my clan, for I would not repeat the cycle nor any in my bloodline. As I looked at each face in the room, my job was done. It was now time for me to return. I stretched forth my hand opening my eyes and was immediately transformed arrayed in white and took my place amongst the ancestors and elders. At last I had truly awakened, and my journey was now complete.